consequences...

Consequences

Laurie Depp

consequences...

I'm with the band

Hodder
Children's
Books

A division of Hachette Children's Book

Dreaming

1

I was trying to dance, but my left foot was trapped underneath a bit of railing at the front of the crowd. I must have looked like a dislocated frog or something, all right side and no rhythm. It wasn't the image I'd been aiming for, but I tried to appear cool and in control as Andy grinned a toothy grin at me and I felt the growing excitement in the sounds that swirled around us.

'God I love you, Ellie!' he shouted, actually aiming it at the sky not me. It sounded something like 'Grod a luff bug hell' by the time it got to me, because the music was pounding between us and the lights obscured his mouth. It didn't really matter, because we'd finally made it to the V festival, together with all our mates: Dylan, Jamie, Kate – and it was the best Saturday night there'd ever been, ever.

I looked behind me, doing little one-legged jumps up and down, trying to see to the back of the crowd in the insane dancing of the strobe lights, trying to get a grip on the scale of it.

Yeah, like that was ever going to happen: there were so

many people moving just like me that I couldn't even see beyond the group of lads right behind us with their shirts wrapped around their heads.

'I love you too, Andy . . .' I screamed, throwing my arms around his neck and being pulled towards him, his strength finally freeing me from my temporary little prison.

I looked up at the huge stage in front of me in wonder. The Last Kiss were on fire tonight. They were tearing through their first single as if there was no tomorrow, and for all I cared, there wouldn't be. This was as perfect as it got.

I grinned at Dylan to my left: he was buzzing on the dope he'd scored earlier in the day when we first arrived. I pulled him down into the bear hug that Andy and I had been sharing and nuzzled both their sweaty heads into my own, suddenly getting lifted off the ground by them in the process.

'I love both of you,' I screeched. 'And it'll be me up there next year! And you,' I shouted, just as they started to push me further up towards their shoulders, laughing together at how easy it was to lift me. 'Don't drop me, whatever you do . . .' I screamed.

I was a bit worried about breaking my neck, but I knew the TV cameras always focused in on girls who were up on guys' shoulders in the crowd. How tragic would it be to get dropped just at that perfect moment when they focused in on my face for the sing-along chorus at the end?

I looked back down and saw my best friends all around me, my band. I took in the crowd at last, finally getting a sense of proportion. We were caught up in a swaying lump of humanity as far as the eye could see.

I turned to the stage and grinned like a mad woman and realised that I just couldn't imagine a world without music, without my friends, my band and my dreams.

Nothing before or since had ever made me think it wasn't going to happen for me. And this was just the confirmation. I raised my arms above my head and started to move to the music.

All this really was going to be mine one day, if I wanted it.

And trust me, I did.

2

'You've never said that to me before.'

I could feel Andy's breathing heavy in the warm, thick air of the tent. The sleeping bag felt hot and clammy around us. I sensed the tightness of his body next to mine.

'Said what? What are you on about?'

I didn't know what the hell he was talking about. All I could remember was the music. I was too high on that to try to remember something I might have said.

'You said you loved me. Did you mean it?'

There was near-silence all around us. Every now and then there was a giggle close by, or a grunt as somebody tripped over another tent rope.

In the darkness I tried to conjure up an image of Andy's face in my mind, imagining what he must look like as he lay next to me, eyes wide open, just like mine. Asking that question.

'Well you never asked me before, did you?' I tried to buy some time.

'I didn't ask this time either.' Andy's arm snaked under my back and began to gather my tiny body towards him like a big, strong, bendy ice-cream scoop. I could feel his naked chest hot against mine, pressing me into him. 'Do you?'

'You really have to ask?' I breathed, my nose and mouth pressed tight against the roughness of his stubble.

My hands on his face, I pulled his mouth insistently on to mine, our tongues touching gently. I traced steps down his bare chest and on to his stomach with my fingers.

I felt his body begin to relax beneath my touch.

'No. I don't need to ask.'

Slowly, I increased the pressure, as Andy's fingers circled upwards to caress and stroke me.

I felt myself slipping into a different world altogether.

As Dylan's stubbly face and gorgeous blue eyes flooded and flashed into my mind.

3

Sunday morning looked like those films you used to see at school, the ones about the First World War, when everybody had given up shooting at each other because they were so knackered they couldn't stand up any more: people standing up asleep; backpacks and plastic bags in piles outside tents; friends huddled around tiny open spaces, their tents circled against outsiders. Luckily there was no mud this year, which I had been dreading. Being without my hair straighteners was bad enough, without getting half of Essex up my bum as well.

Jamie woke us all up around eleven with his farting, which had an echoing effect around our little clearing.

'Ewww. Get your stinking arse out of here, Jamie,' Kate howled at him. I imagined her, straggly festival hair in hands, trying her best to protect her nose with both.

I knew just how she felt. I'd known them since we were little kids, and Jamie had always enjoyed tormenting his sister like this. He was a comedian, and he could usually get a smile on everybody's face – apart from Kate's, occasionally. I heard a slapping noise and a thump and the rustle of a tent that was being pushed to its limits by too many bodies in too small a space. I felt sorry for Dylan, no doubt trapped there, probably too stoned to move, in-between the two of them.

I called out from inside our tent. 'Just don't light any matches in there, OK?'

I giggled and leaned across to kiss Andy awake with little pecks all over his face. He mumbled something into my dangling strands of jet-black hair.

'Leave me alone, Ell, I'm going to die.'

I looked down at Andy, glowing in the morning sun that was filtering through the orange tent walls. He looked like the Tango Man in his sleeping bag, hair spiky short and his body all wrapped up in a big fat tube of orange polyester. I wanted to snuggle him up for breakfast he was so cute. He'd been working all night on Friday, shop fitting in Manchester (double time and free kebabs made it worth it, so he said), and then we'd driven straight to the festival when he'd got home. He must have been knackered.

'OK, you sleep a bit longer. I'm going to get some bagels or something.' I slid out of the top of our zipped-together sleeping bags and slipped on a white miniskirt and vest top.

'Bagels?' Andy mumbled. 'Mine's a burger. And NOT veggie.'

He turned over on his side, and in a moment had started to breathe heavily again.

It was hot when I got outside, the sun baking the tops of field after field of tents, all the way into the distance. I pulled a few bits of stray grass out of my Les Filles top. I'd only got it on Friday. It had looked great with my boots and hot pants last night, if I said so myself: *très chic*. I'd had quite a few admiring stares.

Only a few people had surfaced so far, and the ultra-bright morning light made me blink. We'd marked our space yesterday with a couple of old bed sheets and Dylan's favourite Leeds United banner from when he was a kid. I found Dylan out of the eggy tent already, making some coffee on a little camping stove outside their tent. He didn't look up. He looked wasted.

'Did you sleep OK?' I asked. He pulled a face into the bubbling pan.

'Yeah, like a log. I had Kate on one side snoring, Jamie on the other farting and then got the munchies at 6 a.m. What do you think?'

I laughed. 'Sorry. Better put an extra spoon of coffee in there then. Might wake you up.'

Dylan crossed his legs and squinted up in my general direction through his out-of-control fringe. I could tell he was still buzzing.

'Last night was sick, wasn't it? Last Kiss were killing it. Do you remember the guitar on "Force Me"? I thought it was going to eat me! Never heard anyone make that sound with a guitar before.'

I don't know where Dyl gets his images from, but they always make perfect sense to me and they end up making great songs too.

'I know. I can't wait to get back home and write. I've got a million ideas for songs just from being here and hearing everybody else. I wish you'd brought your guitar so we could do some now.'

Dylan fiddled with his little camping stove as the water boiled, carefully lowering the pan so he could fill his mug. He was precise, slow and methodical, like he had to concentrate or it would all go wrong. He was totally different when we were on stage: then he was like a maniac running around, like he'd finally come to life.

I noticed his hand was shaking a bit.

'You've always got a million ideas, Ell, and you always want to do them right now.' He smiled and lay back on the grass, his mug steaming beside him in the sunlight. 'Chill for a bit. The songs will still be there when we get home.'

It was Dylan all over. He was so laid back that he wasn't just falling over, he was coming around again, back the other way. I tried to lie down too, but I didn't want to get my white skirt dirty in the dust and I felt like I needed a good wash already. And anyway, it felt awkward to be around Dylan when it was just the two of us. It always did.

He never looked at me when we were talking, not even when we'd just come up with the best song we'd ever written and I was jumping up and down squealing with excitement and trying to hug him. It was no different now. He'd closed his eyes, after avoiding mine for most of the conversation.

I hadn't been alone with him since we'd got to the festival. I fell back into the comfort zone of what we always talked about whenever we were left together: the band.

'Dyl, what's happening with the park gig in August? Have you definitely got the booking? Is it confirmed?'

So many times when Dylan had organised something for the band, everything had gone wrong. I didn't want to sound bitchy, but I couldn't think of anything else to talk about. I felt nervous, something that had been happening more and more recently when I was around him. I was glad he wasn't looking at me; I could feel a really attractive beady sweat-moustache growing right across my top lip.

'It's all happening, there's nothing to worry about,' he grunted.

'You're sure? It's just that that party at No Issue was meant—' I didn't get a chance to finish as Jamie poked his head out of their tent, lanky hair flopping around his face.

'Erm, if there's any planning of secret gigs and shit going on here, you need to let me know. That gig was only supposed to be provisional. You telling me it's confirmed?' Grinning, he reached back into the tent and rummaged around for something. I knew what it would be. Seconds later, there was a glint of metal in his hand.

'OK, you can carry on now.' Jamie held up his MP3 recorder, deliberately emphasising it by dangling it around in the air like it was a mobile that he was trying to get a signal for.

We'd all got used to Jamie's weird habits by now. He was always recording us, taping conversations. His excuse these days was that he was training to be a proper journalist, but actually he'd been doing it for years, long before he'd become a real writer. It was weird, but cool sometimes, especially when he magicked your words into a funny sound clip on our MySpace site that he runs for us, or when a clip of my voice turned up in a sample during one of his DJing shows. He used to say that when we were famous he'd be able to make loads of money out of us. We just used to laugh.

'Ah, OK, best keep quiet about that then, Dyl, eh? In case it leaks to the press.' I joked and nodded in Jamie's direction.

Dylan looked up for a second and then rested his head back on the ground in the sun.

I took a moment to focus on his face. He wasn't great looking, but he made up for it with his personality. Charisma, I think they call it.

I thought I might stick around for a bit instead of hunting down a breakfast bap. I scooted down and turned on my side towards Dyl on the big rug we'd spread out to share the night before, making sure I kept a respectable distance between us. The skirt would have to take its chances.

Chill-out music was drifting across the field from somewhere far away and I could smell bacon cooking in the gentle breeze. The sun glistened through my eyelashes, colliding with Dylan-shaped images and the smell of warm, parched grass. There were worse things to do on a sunny Sunday morning than this. In a couple of moments I fell into a peaceful sleep.

A few seconds later the peace was shattered.

An enormous fart ripped through the sides of Jamie's tent and my eyes shot open to see his upper body framed by the flaps of his tent and an expression of comedy surprise on his mouth.

'Ewwwww!' I shrieked. From inside the tent I heard and felt Kate's pain.

'Jamie, you dirty scumbag, that was right in my face . . .'

Seconds later Kate jumped out of the tent and grabbed my hand in desperation. She pulled me up with one hand whilst pulling on her sandals with the other.

'Come on, Ellie, I need to get out of Man World for a bit. Let's go find somewhere to get a wash.'

I looked back to see Dylan calmly supping his coffee, his eyes open and fixed on the spot I'd just left behind.

4

Finding a tap with fresh running water was almost as hard as getting to the festival had been in the first place.

What me and Kate thought might be a bit of a walk, turned into a grumpy expedition over fields of sweaty half-naked boys (OK, that bit wasn't too bad!) in the hot sun. I wasn't impressed that she'd dragged me away from my Dylan-all-to-myself moment for a start. Then there was the hidden tent pegs and ropes assault course amongst the tightly packed little tents, the midges trying to get their own breakfast from my tasty skin and any number of pushy hippies with their bits of brightly coloured cheesecloth for sale acting like we were in a market in Morocco or something. I felt like I had a hangover, and I suppose in some ways I did have, just without the alcohol beforehand.

After a few moments the two of us settled into a self-imposed silence and my mind started to drift to how we'd all got here in the first place, to the long rainy day last summer when we'd been working all afternoon on a new song in my bedroom.

We'd reached a point of total brain-freeze. Andy was

reading the *NME* on my bed. I was trying to erase a misplaced drum sound on the computer. Typical of Dylan, the idea seemed to come from nowhere.

'Andy, let's do the V festival next year,' he'd said, ignoring me as he always did whenever he got enthusiastic about something that didn't involve me singing.

Andy looked up. 'Yeah, why not, sounds like a plan. Where the hell did that come from?'

I piped up from behind the computer. 'Yeah, that'd be fantastic, Dyl.' I hoped it was a band trip and was pitching for an invite. That was how things usually worked then: no guarantees. I was still trying to convince myself that I could be cool enough to fit in this band of Dylan's, let alone his social life. 'Is it far away?'

I'd heard of the V festival, but didn't really know much about it. 'How much would we be paid for doing it?'

Andy grinned across at Dyl.

'It's a good job you're a brilliant singer, Ell,' he laughed. 'When Dyl said "do" the V festival, he was talking about going to watch, not play. It's a big festival. We might not get the gig there for a bit yet.'

They laughed.

OK, so I was naïve, I know. I've grown up a lot since then. They've never let me forget that one though.

After Kate and Jamie said they were in, we had the mad scrap for tickets. I paid up front for everybody else, before I finally got paid back about three-quarters of it by December. Kate wasn't even allowed to go until her parents chilled, after she promised to call them every two hours on her mobile (the one that had mysteriously lost its charge yesterday lunchtime, about ten minutes after we got here). They were well rich, but Kate and Jamie used to have a lot more problems getting to do anything than the rest of us. I'd had a big argument with my dad about the dangers of teenagers being exposed to drug culture. So ironic. I thought about my mum sitting at home right now. I'd been more worried about leaving her on her own for two days, knowing she might take too many of her happy pills while I was gone, than I ever was about myself. I made a mental note to call her as soon as we'd found a tap and had a wash.

After all the arguments with Dad, getting here was simple, apart from 1) Dylan and 2) the transport. When we picked Dylan up, I didn't expect that we'd have to remind him where we were going, as well as wait for him to pack. It was so typical. He'd been working at the club the night before, got loaded, and it had 'slipped his mind' he was going to the V festival. Yeah, that's what I thought too.

Andy had sorted the transport by getting his work's van for the weekend without telling the boss that the 'F and A Braithwaite Fitters' vehicle would be parked in a field in Essex for the weekend. So it was an interesting journey: in a blacked-out van, perching on long slabs of plasterboard that kept rubbing white dust off on my black House of Holland shirt and trying really hard not to fall off every time we went round a corner.

It was actually pretty special that we'd made it there as a

group at all. I know my dad wouldn't think so and he'd probably do anything he could to keep me away from their 'bad influence', as he called it, but I love all of my mates to bits, and I think we're a pretty special bunch of people.

5

Kate stopped for a minute beside a New Age fortune-teller's tepee.

'I need a breather,' she laughed. 'Too many fags.' She hacked a couple of major coughs out, as if to prove the point.

I frowned sympathetically. I'd given up when I started singing seriously. The two things didn't mix. I put my hand on her back to try and comfort her, scanning the horizon for signs of any washing facilities at all.

'I can see a line of people about half a field away. At this rate I reckon we could make it by sundown. I recognise the flag down there. They've definitely got bogs.'

I'd been yesterday. I didn't tell her what state the toilets were in.

Kate looked up and scowled.

'Cheeky bitch! It's all your fault anyway, this. If you hadn't decided to join BlackStar and be Andy's girlfriend and secretly lust after Dyl, you and me would be back home in Leeds drinking cocktails and sitting next to our pool right now. Smelling of Dolce and Gabbana and feeling very clean. Grrrr . . .'

I laughed again. She was right in so many ways. I couldn't believe that I was stood at a rock festival, a couple of fields away from my boyfriend, who I'd just shared a night of passion with in our shared tent. So much of that was mind-blowing compared to the life of Ellie Batchelor pre-BlackStar. Thank God for Dyl and Andy, I thought.

I'd been the perfect little overachieving daughter back then: all A*s on my school reports, piles of fluffy teddies drowning my duvet and trophies from endless singing competitions lining the bedroom shelves. I felt like a different person now, and it was all down to Andy and Dylan.

It was back in Year Eleven that I'd first met the lads.

Kate and I went to the same school, so when my parents split I started spending more time with her and Jamie. Dyl and Andy were Jamie's best mates. He knew them from doing gigs and DJing.

We all started hanging out at the park and then going to parties and down to the pub, which helped me escape from what was going on at home, which was a bit shit. We'd talk about music, but at that stage it was always in the background. And then, when we finally did play together, everything just sort of clicked.

Dyl wasn't sure at all about me at first, let alone my music. I don't know if he'd even discovered what he'd got in his boxers by then, but he never seemed to notice I was a girl, let alone one that was trying to get his attention. Andy did, but I just saw him as a big cuddly mate.

I remember the first thing Dylan ever said to me. It was

at the park, on the hill that we all used to lie on at night in the summer to look at the stars.

'You're called what?' He snorted.

'Elliana.' I repeated my name for him, hoping he'd never forget it, or at least not make fun of it.

'What kind of name is that? You can't be called that if you're from Leeds. That's like me being called Jeremy or Tarquin or something.'

My face burned hot. Luckily it was nearly dark, so nobody saw.

'I'm part Spanish,' I managed to squeak out. 'My mum's side. It's a Spanish name.'

And that was pretty much the way things went between us for a bit.

I saw a little girl perched on her mum's lap singing outside their tent, and I remembered with a smile how everything had changed for all of us on the day I sang with the lads for the first time, a couple of months after we met.

I'd overheard Dylan and Jamie talking about me one day with Andy, when they thought Kate and I had gone downstairs for some more beer from the fridge. I'd stopped off at the toilet on the way, and hovered at the bedroom door instead of carrying on down to help Kate.

'I've heard her, mate, you should give her a try.' I heard Jamie's voice.

'Look, she went to a girls' school, man,' Dylan was saying. 'She's cool, but she's not gonna be able to do much more than sing in tune with a posh accent, is she? No offence, Andy, but you know what I mean, don't you?'

Andy didn't reply.

I knew why Dylan thought like that. He'd already worked out correctly that I'd been one of those girls who did dance, drama school, music lessons, guides, choir, sometimes all in the same evening. And he'd heard me talk to Andy about how my dad pushed me, even more so since the divorce, not letting me pull out of anything if I was tired. Dad said I had too much talent to chuck it away by not working hard to fulfil it. It felt like Venus and Serena's dad, without the tennis rackets and the grunting.

'I really think you should get her to sing some of your stuff, Dyl,' Jamie said. 'She's wicked: white Latino girl, black voice. I can see the press release for your first album now.'

Andy agreed with Jamie. 'When they come back let's play her the Looney Tubes tape, yeah, Dyl? We need to get some proper vocals on that. I heard Ellie singing along to her iPod the other day and she sounded great. And I think any girl doing vocals has gotta be better than you doing it.'

Dylan joined in with the laughter.

'Yeah true, good point. All right, we'll see if she wants to give it a go.'

Later on, after hatching a secret plan with Kate that involved flirty dancing and lots of singing with eye contact, I'd come back and proved Jamie and Andy right.

I looked at Kate now, slummy jeans and boho top all floaty in the breeze, still trying to get her breath back while lighting another fag from her quickly dwindling pack, and I thanked her silently for giving me that extra bit of confidence I'd needed to go back and pass my 'audition'.

It had all come at just the right time for me, giving me even more excuses to avoid my parents and making me feel I actually belonged somewhere at last.

So I agreed to join the band. They were called something different then (Fugwumpers or something else stupid), but once I'd brought the computer and some beautiful singing to the party, we changed the name. BlackStar was my idea too.

And the rest is history, as they say.

Except that there was just a wee bit more to it than that.

I'd actually started going out with Andy before I got in the band. It wasn't long before, but it did mean that our relationship was always going to have an effect on the band and how we worked together: that was obvious, good or bad. Maybe it had an influence on Andy giving me a chance to sing for Dylan too, I don't know. I decided I'd rather not know.

My mind drifted back to Dylan lying flat out in the Glastonbury sun a few minutes before. If only he knew what a mess he was making of my head these days.

And then there was last night with Andy in the tent. It had been amazing, so sexy, but it was all a bit wrong, but too easy to do nothing about. I just had to keep myself under control, like I always did. All those years living around my super-controlling dad had at least prepared me for that.

How did I get myself into this mess?

It happened a few days before I sang with Dyl and Andy for the first time. It was late one evening and we were all in the park, having a go on the kids' playground roundabout thing.

By the time I'd gone round a few times my three WKDs were kicking in, so Andy stopped the ride and looked after me while the others went on the slides. And then it happened: I was trying to watch Dylan as he wobbled drunkenly down the slide when Andy kissed me really gently but with his big, clumsy hands on my face, and I was hooked in. It was my first proper kiss, and it was gorgeous, and I'd never felt so loved in all my life. I felt tears of something (gratitude maybe, or relief? I can't even imagine it now) start to form in my eyes right in the middle of it, but I managed to hold them in, so Andy never saw.

I'd hoped it would be Dylan kissing me like that, but he never gave me any attention when we weren't talking about music or where his next joint was coming from. Andy talked to me and listened when I moaned about my parents. He helped calm me down when I got emotional and said I wanted to carve out my dad's heart and roast it on a spit.

So that was it: one kiss and we were together and we'd been like that ever since. My head was slightly mashed, of course, and I used to wonder how I could change what I'd never wanted to start, but I never did find an answer. Andy was so kind and gentle, so thoughtful, even though his own life had been totally crap: his mum died when he was little and his dad turned into an alcoholic. I soon realised that I was probably giving him more support than he was giving me, but by then it was all too late to go back.

6

Kate snapped me back to attention from my daydream.

'What's up with you, Ell? You look like you're a million miles away. What you dreaming about now? Another night with Andy?'

She elbowed me gently in the ribs.

'Like we all didn't hear you last night anyway.'

'Nooo,' I said, blushing. 'Oh God, how embarrassing.' I forced a gulped laugh and changed the subject. 'No, I'm just thinking about all of us and how great it is to be here with everyone. It'll never change, will it?' I asked her. 'We'll be friends always, whatever happens, won't we?'

'God, take a chill pill. Have you taken some of Dylan's stash? We're definitely not going to be friends forever if we don't get moving now. That mystical Ouija board mad woman over there with the beard is starting to look like she's interested in us.'

'OK, let's get moving,' I agreed, giggling.

We reached the Portaloos and had a quick pee and then took the opportunity to have a bit of a quick bikinied-underarm-and-face-wash at the taps next door. We must have looked really quite attractive in our bikini tops and shorts as we were rubbing our pits. Kate was scrubbing away like mad, still on a bit of an adrenaline high from the night before, although more practical matters were starting to trouble her.

'Ell, I really need to find somewhere to go that doesn't stink like a sewer,' she said quietly, surrounded as we were by lots of sweaty, unwashed people waiting their turn for our tap. 'I need to poo and I'm not going back in one of those.' She nodded towards the Portaloos. 'I held my breath the whole time I was in there. It made me feel sick. And you know what I'm like when I can't go for a poo.'

'Err, Kate? Hello? Too much information. . . .' I frowned randomly in her general direction.

We'd shared a lot of crises over the years, although usually they were more emotional than toilet moments. There had been many times when Kate had cried in my arms, not always drunkenly, over boyfriends, exam pressure, parents not letting her go out late, you name it. It had always seemed a bit weak to me, crying like that, but that hadn't stopped me helping, because she was my mate.

We giggled. Girls at festivals were rubbish, me included. We're not built for it. Kate had always been a girlie girl, just like me. And I didn't want her in a bad mood all day. I knew it would be catching.

'OK, you're in luck,' I whispered. 'This is the same toilet block where I had a pee yesterday, 'cept I didn't use the loos at all. Me and this girl got talking and we got the security people to let us go in a field over there. Have you got your bog roll?'

I winked as Kate nodded quizzically and patted her little supply bag, and I dragged her away from the lovely cold tap we'd been hogging for minutes on end. I thought about the girl I'd met, Becky, and the conversation we'd had the day before, just at this spot. I'd finally found a good moment to tell Kate about it, away from the boys.

'This girl, Becky, she is a journalist from London. She said she knew somebody at *Pop World*, you know, the thing I went and auditioned for, for TV? She said she'd put a good word in for me. I really hope she comes through. It was so weird that we met like that.'

Kate stopped and looked me right in the eyes.

'Wow, Ellie, that's so cool. An inside connection.' She smiled, then paused for a second. 'But is this *Pop World* stuff what you really want? I mean, Jamie and I have been talking about it since you went for the audition. What if the boys find out? And what about BlackStar?'

None of these questions were new. I'd been asking myself them for weeks.

'And what if you actually get through? You know Dylan and Andy hate TV talent shows. Dylan told Jamie last week that he'd cut the balls off anybody he ever met who'd been on one. And that's Dylan. Imagine what Andy would be like.'

Bless. She was so concerned about me.

'Well it's a good job I don't have any balls then, isn't it?' I joked, trying to lighten the mood. 'And what they don't know won't hurt them for now. I mean, I know the audition went well, but who knows if I'll get into the last sixteen. These things are down to who you know, not how good you are. But I have to do it, Kate, you know I've been trying to get somewhere with my music forever, and Dylan and Andy aren't exactly pushing it with the band right now, are they?'

Kate looked down, her blonde highlights catching in the sun.

'Well, Dyl's deferred uni for it at least,' she said. 'I know he's a pisshead, but at least he did that. You never know, he could actually get his act together this year.'

I laughed. The thought of Dylan actually being properly committed to anything was too funny.

'And the thing is,' Kate continued, 'I just don't like lying to Dyl and Andy, neither does Jamie, and even though I know you're doing it for their sakes in case nothing comes of it, it still makes me nervous.'

I took Kate's hands in mine and held them tight.

'Look, until I put a rocket up Dylan's backside, BlackStar is going to carry on being a "quite popular band" around Leeds with nobody else taking the slightest bit of interest in us. I might dream of starring at Glastonbury next year with the band, but right now I need to try other things, give myself a chance while I can, before my dad makes me into his little corporate lawyer and the band falls apart. You know I have to do it. We talked about this before.'

Kate squeezed my hands back.

'I know what you're saying, Ell. And you know I'm right behind you.'

She tried to hold her 'deeply serious' look for more than a split second, but failed, breaking into a grimacing smile instead. 'But can you show me where I can go to the toilet now? If you don't there could be a nasty accident right behind me.'

7

From: jmeex@hotmail.com
To: cityvision@randombiz.net
Subject: Glastonbury 2008 – E-zine report copy

Sam, let me know if you need to make changes
before uploading: I've linked the V and Leeds
festivals as you suggested. I'll check email at the
café on Sunday PM. Leaving here midnight. Got
some great pics of the band to upload later . . . Ellie
in pink sombrero and bikini! Cya
Jamie

TRASHION VICTIMS? – BLACKSTAR: IT'S DAYLIGHT ROBBERY AT THE V FESTIVAL

It was a parade of the tragically hip that
led them to the Vorlex Stage on Saturday
night, but once they were there BlackStar
finally brought a sense of style to the
place. The proto-hippies didn't know what
had hit them.

The super-hottest young band in the
North was all the way down here to show

everybody else the way: and all around them there were signs of impending world domination, from the mobile phone masts that pierced the sky and adverts for new albums by international super 'stars', to the power trailers for BBC execs and presenters paid by the dumper truck to pretend to be now.

BlackStar rose above it all majestically.

OK, so this year they were just watching, but next time, who knows? They really are that good.

I watched them love the festival experience from close quarters, and I can tell you now that this band knows how to party. Soon enough I predict they'll be back to take over. Remember what I told you about the Kaisers not so long ago?

You've read about BlackStar before here, after their fusion of electronic R'n'B and guitar pop blasted its way into this city's consciousness with loaded gigs at the Roundmill and the Sound and Vision in the last couple of months.

Before that the word-of-mouth recommendations were coming in from the student crowd, kids at Underage nights and on the net. Their MySpace site has had

10,000 hits and counting and, I'm told, a sneaky bit of attention from some of the bigger regional promoters looking to catch a new wave of talent from the Leeds area.

And now the rumours of a real festival showcase are confirmed. No, not Glastonbury, that can wait: BlackStar today confirmed to me that they will join the five other confirmed acts at Daylight Robbery in the Park, showcasing on the main stage on 28 August, Bank Holiday Monday.

The buzz is growing, and it's surely only a matter of time before this translates into a deal (if they want one). Some might say it's better for them to keep it DIY. It's worked before – just look at the Arctic Monkeys – and for Dylan, Ellie and Andy, whose latest tracks can be heard by clicking on the links to the left of this article, there's no question that they want to stick to what they believe.

Dylan Patrick, main songwriter and guitarist, told us: 'Why would we want to sell out to some huge multinational record company, when we can distribute our stuff on the web and build up a fan base there, like we already have? There's nothing in it for me if it's all about money and product. I only care about the music, playing live and recording.'

Dylan's got strong opinions. He loved the Glastonbury experience, but he had plenty to say about the way the festival has gone in recent years.

'I was talking to this guy who'd been going for years; he said that the whole thing was becoming a media circus, not the music festival it was and what it should be. He probably won't be coming next year. Maybe a lot of people will feel like that. We saw a lot of that crap around the edges too, but when we were watching the music, that was what made it special. Everything else is just hype.'

Ellie Batchelor, lead singer and dusky North Leeds/Mediterranean fashionista, has the last word on BlackStar's ambitions: 'I want to play Glastonbury, V, all the festivals, and we're gonna go for it from now on, concentrating totally on the writing and the gigging. We're excited to be doing Daylight Robbery. We've been going to watch now for a couple of years, so to be up on stage will be amazing. And imagine in five years' time: you wouldn't want to have to say you missed us when we started out, would you? How sad would that be?'

You've been warned: Daylight Robbery in the Park: Victoria Park, Leeds, 28 August: don't miss it!

8

My Bedroom   3 a.m.   Monday

Andy,

I can't even believe I'm writing this. I can't sleep and u only dropped me off about half an hour ago, but I've been thinking so much recently, especially this weekend, and I have to get it all out. I can't tell u to ur face or email u or text u or any of that. I just want u to know there are 2 things that I haven't told u about and I can't hold it in any more. U need to know. I'm really hoping u will tell Dyl for me as well, Andy, cos I don't think I can. I'm a total wuss.

Uv been everything to me for the last 2 years and I feel like shit for keeping stuff from u. Like, when my parents were splitting, u always used to tell me that ud look after me, and even tho' I told u I didn't need looking after, just caring 4, but u still did it and I got used 2 it and liked it. And it was the same with the band. Whenever Dyl was being a knob u always made sure I didn't lose it and get into fights with him. I knew u were helping, even tho' I never thanked u. So thank u. SOOO much. I mean it.

Anywayz, here goes: shit this is so hard. Ok, the 1st thing I need to tell u is that I've had an audition 4 this TV thing called Pop World. I know ur gonna hate this and Dyl 2, but I might get in and I could be going away 4 a bit if i do. And it's a talent show thing. I know, but u know what I want 2 do and that if I don't do it soon my dad'll force me to go 2 work as a lawyer and I can't face that yet. I have 2 try for this at least. And Dyl isn't gonna get his ass into gear anytym soon is he?

Ok second thing. This is harder. I don't want u to get the wrong idea here, but u need to know.

When we 1st met I fancied Dyl but I liked u more and when we kissed it was amazing and lovely and I've loved every second of the last 2 years with u. But . . .

I put my pen down and stared at the piece of lined A4 school paper.

Who was I trying to kid? As if I could ever send this. How to ruin one person's life in twenty lines of writing. I didn't have the heart. Or the nerve. Or the balls.

I screwed it up and chucked it in the waste paper basket by my desk.

9

Waking up back in Leeds was horrible. Or rather, waking up at home was horrible.

If it wasn't bad enough that I'd just had the greatest weekend of my life, I knew what I would have to face when I finally crawled out from under my duvet and that it would be a lot worse than when I left.

Mum was in the living room, where she always is, when I finally got up late in the afternoon, after zoning out for practically two whole days. I was hanging on a call from *Pop World*. They'd said they would call by the end of August, because they had auditions all over the country and mine was the first, but I'd convinced myself that I would hear sooner: part of my Batchelor 'confidence' maybe. Some would call it arrogance. There was still three weeks of summer to go before that, but every time I woke up from my festival exhaustion haze I checked my phone, convinced I might have missed them. Every time I was disappointed.

'Are you OK, Mum?' I asked, without expecting much of a response.

She looked up at me slowly, as if trying to recognise who

it was that had invaded her silence and the flickering of *Homes under the Hammer* on the TV screen.

'Oh, Elliana.'

Mum always used my full Spanish name. I think it was her way of getting back at Dad. 'You've been away so long. I was wondering if you'd ever come back.' She smiled weakly. If it wasn't my mum talking, I would've thought she was being sarcastic, but Mum didn't do sarcasm, she was usually too dosed up. I knew she actually meant it.

'Mum, I was only away for a couple of days. I've been asleep since I got back. You saw me on Monday morning, remember? When you woke me up and I shouted at you?' I smiled affectionately and crouched down beside her in the armchair. 'We had an amazing time at the festival, Mum. It was wicked. I got to see loads of bands and we stayed up all night on Saturday just talking and chilling. I wish you could've come.'

I didn't really, obviously, but Mum needed to know somebody cared about her.

'Darling, would you mind getting me a cup of tea? I've been thinking about having one for a while now.' She leaned in towards me as if telling me a secret. 'I'd really like to telephone your aunty and talk to her but I don't suppose she'll be around at this time. It's late. She never has time for me now, anyway.'

Mum always wanted to talk to her sister. Trouble was, Aunt Gabriela was a consultant heart surgeon at the main hospital in Barcelona. She was never in, even when my mum had the energy to try. And my mum was right: she didn't have time for her little sister Isabella.

I was worried about my mum. I'd been worried about her for years, but it had started to get a lot worse recently. When my dad had had to move out after the divorce, and my mum got the house even though he had tried everything to stop her, he'd been trying anything to make her state of mind more fragile.

'Look, you just sit there and I'll get you a nice cup of tea and a couple of Jaffa Cakes. Then we can go for a walk down to the park or something? If you want to?'

I tried to look enthusiastic. I felt guilty about it, but I wasn't in the mood to walk at a mile an hour down our road with my mum looking like a geriatric, but she needed to get out for a bit. Depression is almost as bad when you're next to it as when you have it. As if it wasn't enough having to prop Dylan up when he doped himself up, now my mum was turning into a basket case too.

Just then the doorbell went. Something clenched up in me: I knew it must be Dad. Nobody else ever came round to ours unannounced. I always made my mates call ahead so I could get my mum settled and out of the way.

Dad was clutching something to his chest when I saw him through the glass panes of the big old door. It was a folder full of papers.

'Oh you're back, then? Didn't have time to call your dad yet? What do I pay that mobile contract for anyway? I never get anything back from it.'

Dad was tall and powerfully built, short fair hair cropped into a very English style. He was very northern looking, alternating between pale- and red-faced, quite the opposite of me and mum. I'd inherited Mum's olive skin and dark eyes and we were both quite petite. They say opposites attract. I assumed that must have been the only thing that ever brought them together at university when they met. All the evidence since proved that they had very little in common.

I tried to smile a greeting, aware that his mood didn't sound that bad today, if you ignored the sarcasm.

'Dad, I've been sleeping for the last two days. It's tiring being a festival-goer you know. You must remember from the sixties?'

He faked a punch at my arm. 'I was only just born in the bloody sixties, thank you very much. You kids are just lightweights anyway. We used to do all-nighter soul weekends at the end of a working week. None of your sleeping in tents for us.'

I could cope with Dad when he was in this kind of mood. It was just when he started on Mum. It was horrible. If I could just keep between him and the living room we might be all right.

'So have you brought me a pressie?' I glanced down at the folder in his hand, hoping that it wasn't some kind of legal paper for him to shout at my mum about yet again. Ever since he'd left two years ago, he usually had something for me when he came: 'guilt trip gifts' as I called them. Usually pretty good stuff, actually.

'Yep I have. Do you want to come for a coffee and a chat down at the parade?'

I was tempted for a split second but then realised I couldn't leave my mum for him now. It would cause too many problems later trying to make it up to her.

'No, I can't, I've just promised to take Mum for a walk down there in a bit. Why don't you come in and have a drink here in the garden. I'll take Mum out later on.'

Dad nodded and looked a bit exasperated. He was never keen on fitting in around us, especially Mum.

Once I'd made us coffee, we sat outside in the garden of the home they'd made together for twenty years. It was always weird when he came back. All I could think of were the lovely days when he would play Frisbee with me all day on the lawn all those summers ago, when things seemed so perfect, and Mum would make fresh lemonade in big jugs with ice and fruit and he would call me his 'princess'; or the times when he was shouting at her because she'd just discovered his latest dirty little affair with some secretary from work or other. Those days weren't quite so good.

By the time I was twelve I just tried to keep out of the way and not get caught in the middle. I couldn't stand how he treated her, but I couldn't seem to stop wanting to please him. He was my dad after all.

'So I have something for you,' he began, reaching into the envelope folder on his lap. 'It's pretty special, and I want you to think long and hard about it.' He gave me one of his hard stares, the kind he reserved for moments when he had high expectations of me. 'I've been worried that you were going to waste your time with that band and do nothing all year, so I've got something for you to do in your spare time.'

I took the papers without replying and started to read. What had he cooked up for me now?

Mason, Batchelor and Soames
International Corporate Law Partnership
I Upper Parliament Street
Leeds LS1 2JG

<u>Formal Offer of Temporary Internship Contract</u>

For: Elliana Batchelor

Job Description:
- Working exclusively on the Grant International, Fortune Inc., Beattie and Toller accounts, acting as full-time Legal Assistant to Deacon Mason, Chief Partner.
- Salary: 75% basis of current legal profession rates.
- Opportunities to work at the Bar, in Chambers and with clients on a fully integrated, equivalence basis.
- In-service training provided on all Corporate Law aspects at head office.
- Regular attendance at international meetings required. (Copenhagen, Milan and New York)
- Liaison with all partners on client matters, including

attendance at Partnership Board meeting level.
- On favourable completion, priority given to any future application for employment in the practice.

Acceptance of Contract:
Signed (On behalf of the company): Deacon Mason
Signed (Elliana Batchelor):

I looked back over what I'd just read. I couldn't believe it. This was an offer beyond anyone's wildest dreams (if they had wild dreams about becoming a solicitor). It was working at a level above even that of a trainee who had already gone to uni. I was only just out of school and hadn't even got my A-level results yet. My dad had really pulled some strings to sort this one out.

It was horrible.

'Dad, this is amazing. How did you get them to agree to all that?' I said, trying to buy some time before I had to detonate the bomb that would be my father's head when I said no.

He smiled. Peter Batchelor was nothing if not modest, at least not in his own mind. He gave a little snort, as if to say 'you really have to ask?'. It wasn't the most attractive feature of my dad's, and it gave me some courage for the fight.

'I spoke about you to Deacon, and he's got contacts at your school through the Round Table and down in Bristol at the university. Apparently your interview there was outstanding. Everybody has said you're worth it, even me.'

He grinned. He was always saying I was worth stuff, usually to make me work harder to prove him right.

'I can't believe it. It's like a proper job. There are people coming out of Law School that would kill for a job like this. Thanks so much for doing this for me.' I stalled again as the words came out but my brain engaged elsewhere. How could I possibly turn this down when everybody he worked with had helped him put it together? There was only one thing that might help. I swallowed hard and began.

'Dad, you know why I took the year out in the first place, to actually give my music a proper chance? You supported me on that.' He looked like he was about to butt in, so I ploughed on quickly. 'I know you're not that keen on BlackStar, but you've always said I had the talent and you've pushed me all the way with my singing. You've always said that if I could get to the very top with that you wouldn't mind me giving up on the law or uni, but that I had to prove myself. Remember you even said you'd pay for Stage School when I was thinking about going to London, well until the div—'

I paused for a second to regroup. Maybe now wasn't the best time to mention the 'big split' and everything he'd lost in the settlement. At least it kept Dad quiet for a second too.

'Well I've got this chance to do something else. I haven't told you about it yet because at the moment I'm waiting for it to be definite. But it could be everything I always wanted. Mum doesn't even know. You know what she's like about me not going to uni. You've always been the supportive one about all that.'

This wasn't so bad after all. You could make anything sound positive to anybody if you just used the right words. Perhaps I should be a lawyer after all?

'What is it?' Dad never said much when he didn't have to. I could sense a growling in his tone though.

'*Pop World*. I've had an audition. They said I'm on the list and they'll call me back. That means I'm close to the final thirty-two. If I get through that I'll be on TV every week till Christmas. I know I could win it and then I could be anything, get right to the top, like I said I would when you supported my year out.'

I paused again and looked down, waiting for the explosion. There was an uneasy silence from the other side of the table and I daren't look up.

'And what about this "band" you're always going on about?' Dad squeezed the word out like he was chewing on a particularly unpleasant-tasting piece of food. 'Where do they fit in?'

Dad had never like Dylan and Andy. He said it was because he could smell the dope whenever they were around, but I figured it was more to do with the estate they came from.

'They don't,' I said. 'It's just me doing this. They don't know anything about it.'

And as if by magic the atmosphere changed. Suddenly I was aware of a different dad in front of me.

46

'That's my girl. I knew you'd come to your senses about all that.'

I smiled as if I was agreeing with him.

'If you think you're nearly there with this audition, then I'm with you all the way. The internship can wait. I can hold it until you know. I was just trying to push you along and get you moving in the right direction anyway, but you seem to have done that for yourself.' He smiled warmly, and I felt a strange sense that this had all gone a bit too well to be right. 'Maybe all those years we spent winning those song and dance competitions will be worth it after all.'

We? We! I thought he'd just driven the car and held my 'Double-Your-Lashes' mascara and my dangly competition ID card.

'I always knew you were a chip off the old block, Ellie.'

10

Mum didn't take the promise of *Pop World* quite so well.

By the time she'd finished crying and saying that I was throwing away all my opportunities to get out of Leeds and away from my father and find out what I really wanted out of life by going to a good university, I was exhausted and she had very red eyes. She wasn't tough like my dad though, I knew she'd wear out soon enough, and eventually she just gave up and went back to staring at the TV.

That night I went out with the gang to Spirit, the bar/club over in Headingly, needing to clear my head a bit, even though I knew Dylan was working and that would make things more complicated than ever.

Dylan was like the odd-job man at Spirit, except most of his jobs were really important, like being the sound man for all the bands, making sure that Jamie and the other DJs had their systems plugged in to the right socket and making sure the bands were kept 'happy' with all the right substances they needed. He'd been there since the start of Year Twelve, working as many nights as he could and proving himself on the mixing desk to the manager. Now it was like Dylan's little empire, a place he went to live out his own particular dream of the music biz, and he was brilliant at what he did. It wasn't quite what I saw as superstardom and success, it was all a bit grubby and sticky under your shoes, but for Dylan it represented the 'right' way to do things.

Every time I went there he trotted out the same 'amazing' facts about Spirit: Oasis played there when they were just starting out, to a crowd of three and a half people and a dog; The Killers had played a secret gig there before their first V Festival; and somewhere back in the old days David Bowie had done an acoustic set on the same night that Marc Bolan and T-Rex had boogied the place to death.

Personally I was glad it was our club now, because it meant I got to hang out with my friends and check out fit lads when Andy wasn't around.

Sometimes that was the best kind of night, I thought to myself sadly.

It wasn't that Andy and I weren't perfect in some ways, just that he wasn't exactly what I needed in others. I'd kind of fallen for him because he was my knight in shining armour when Dad was throwing dinner plates at the walls and Mum was threatening everything from suicide to chopping off Dad's willy. Sometimes, though, I wondered what it would be like to go out with somebody else, maybe somebody with a more exciting side, or just an exciting side full stop.

Late that evening we were all sitting around in one of the circular booths long after the DJ had finished. It was the usual crew, minus Andy, who'd left earlier: he had to start work at five in the morning. (Dumb job.) So me, Dyl, Jamie and Kate were left to put the world to rights and plan for world domination for BlackStar (or just for me, in case BlackStar's didn't work, I thought to myself).

'Ell, when are you going to get your hair cut? You need to get a new style, for God's sake. That swept-over-the-front thing is so last Tuesday. If I'm going to sell you to my readers, at least you need to give me some attitude with the hair.'

Jamie was always flirting harmlessly with me. Kate said he thought I was one of the lads and I could take it and that he didn't mean anything by it. He saved it for moments when Andy wasn't there though. Andy didn't tolerate the attention I got from other guys very well.

I pretended to give a snooty look down my nose at Jamie. He thought it was messed up that I changed my hairstyle or colour once a month (or more, if we had a lot of gigs). What did he know? I had my public to consider. I gave it my best Paris Hilton.

'J, this from the guy who still has a floppy public school fringe with the spiky-up bit at the back from the eighties? You're not exactly cutting edge, are you? You look like you're in Busted, you saddo.'

Dylan snorted out a laugh and we all looked at him, surprised. It was rare to get so much reaction from him. At least tonight he wasn't totally wasted for a change.

'Are you OK, Dyl?' Kate laughed, deliberately over-surprised.

Dylan nodded in admiration.

'I'm fine, ta. Just enjoying Jamie getting the piss taken out of him. Ell's gonna eat you alive, mate. Quit now.'

'OK, if we're talking about hair,' Jamie continued, turning to Dylan, 'when are you gonna get over the whole urban-troubadour-Dylan-in-1963 thing that your dad forced you into when he named you? At least Ell's hair is in this millennium.'

Dylan acted a little hurt for a minute, before turning to Jamie with a rare glint in his eye.

'I think you're just a bit too bothered about hair, mate.' He paused. 'Specially Ell's hair. You're supposed to be the sophisticated journalist and DJ that knows everything about everything, aren't you? And you shouldn't be looking anyway. It's obvious you fancy her. Maybe I'll mention it to Andy and then he'll come over to your posh house and roast your nuts for breakfast for trying to get with his girl.'

Dylan picked up his beer bottle and took a swig in triumph. Kate cheered, surprised. It was the longest we'd heard Dylan speak for about a year.

Before Jamie could protest, I swung a thump in Dylan's direction.

'As if, Dyl. You're such a stirrer, you are. You just sit there all night not speaking and being mysterious, and then come out with a load of crap to try and get Jamie into trouble.' I turned back to Jamie as he knocked back some lager from his glass, deliberately speaking louder. 'It's OK, Jamie, I know he's bullshitting.' I grinned at each of them in turn.

'I know that if there's anybody fancies me in this world, it's Dyl.'

Dylan's face dropped for a second, as Jamie just managed to avoid spraying us all with a mouthful of beer. Dylan put his head in hands and pretended to cry.

'Nice one, Ell, I love it,' Jamie gasped.

I laughed at them both as they shook hands, accepting defeat.

Jamie piped up again. 'The thing is, it's probably true. He only let you join the band cos he thought you had a good rack. That's what he told me, anyway.'

'Yeah, yeah, keep it up if you can,' I laughed. 'You know I will destroy you completely if you carry this on.'

Jamie and I giggled into our drinks again.

Dylan held up his bottle and we all clinked the glass together. Dylan avoided my eyes as usual, but I could tell he was enjoying the crack.

I did notice that he'd gone a bit red though.

11

From: jmeex@hotmail.com
To: billglaister@leedsmercury.com
Subject: Daylight Robbery in the Park festival –
report copy

Bill,

It's Monday, just got back. Copy for the festival this weekend attached. Hope you like it. It's come in at 300 words as requested. I've made sure it's understandable for all you old people and the more 'mature' reader he he! Syndicating in modified form for audiences to *Yorkshire Echo* and the local zines as agreed.

Black Stars!

It was a real homecoming at Victoria Park yesterday, when some of our best up-and-coming local bands took over the Daylight Robbery festival for a Bank

Holiday celebration of Leeds' vibrant music scene.

In front of more than five thousand excited fans, Bullet, Line King, The Edge of Reason, Holy Molly and BlackStar took to the stage, and the sun beat down on what was a perfect day to end the summer.

All the bands were impressive: Line King deserve particular praise for their driving brand of power pop, whilst Holy Molly rocked out late in the afternoon in hardcore style.

But the eclectic mix was brought to a perfect conclusion when the light began to fade and BlackStar took to the stage. Drifting R 'n' B beats juxtaposed with chiming Rickenbacker guitar melodies opened their set, setting the tone for that end-of-summer, aching sense of loss sensation that we all feel at this time of year.

It could have been downtown Manhattan, a street party on 125th and 3rd, with the stunning combination of Ellie Batchelor's sultry lead vocals, Dylan Patrick's shimmering soundscapes and Andy Moffat's dancing bass rhythms.

But this was Leeds. And like Lily Allen's homages to London, BlackStar's *lyrics firmly place this outstanding band here in the North of England, especially on 'Why Would I Go?', with its images of Harvey Nicks on a Saturday lunchtime, the urban chic young scene in the bars of the city and fish and chips with your boyfriend at the back of the market.*

Don't wait too long for BlackStar. The A and R men were everywhere at Daylight Robbery, and with all due respect to the other bands there, everybody knew why. It's only a matter of time before our next great band gets the attention they deserve.

12

Backstage afterwards was electric. We just couldn't come down off the natural high.

We didn't have a trailer or any kind of room, just a little cordoned-off area that had our name attached to the ribbon with a bit of paper, but with the lights and the noise of dismantling the stage going on around us, it felt like our dressing room anyway, a private space to go a bit mad in with the excitement.

'Dyl, you were fantastic tonight. Never seen you like that before, mate,' Andy grinned. 'I thought you were gonna fall off that speaker stack at one point.'

Dylan laughed self-consciously.

'I don't know what came over me,' he said in a girly fake voice, jumping up and down and running his hands through long sweaty hair, gathering it up and then letting it fall over and over. It was so funny. He looked like he had a head twitch, he was so animated. 'I think I've got a split personality.'

His face was glowing with the excitement. Tonight we'd nailed it, the two of us. We'd always had a good stage presence together, but that had been something else: electricity; chemistry; whatever you called it, it was special. I'd never seen him looking so fit. If only he could be like this all the time. Suddenly I caught myself. I remembered that Andy was right there.

'It was amazing though. I can't believe we got two encores. I thought we were gonna have to do the same songs twice cos we were running out.'

Dyl plonked himself down on one of our white plastic patio chairs and let out a huge sigh of contentment.

I caught his eye as I went under our table to get a bottle of water, just for a split second before he looked away. Too long for him. Not for me. I had to stop feeling like this. It was getting to be a problem.

I quickly turned to Andy, but my phone went off again. It hadn't stopped flashing up new texts since we came off stage. Even in the middle of BlackStar's greatest moment, I was still checking every text to make sure it wasn't from *Pop World*. That told me something. I was pretty sure it wouldn't be them now, not at this time of night. Or maybe it would. I'd heard stories about people finding out that they'd got in in the weirdest ways. But it didn't look like that would ever happen to me. I was starting to resign myself to being stuck to the side of a big-shot solicitor for the next year, writing songs in my bedroom with BlackStar when or if I had some spare time. At least we could still do gigs like this though. That would be something.

'It's Jamie,' I read from my phone. 'He's sorted out some

kind of after-party for all the bands and their mates at Spirit. He's on his way already. Didn't want to tell us before the gig, in case we bombed. Cheeky get!'

Just then I became aware of somebody standing at the edge of our area. Nobody had bothered us since the organiser hugged and slapped us all on the back as we came off the stage, and in our excitement we'd almost forgotten that the rest of the world existed. Only now did the figure step forward out of the shadows. He was wearing a beige linen suit and a collarless shirt, probably Zara, something my dad might wear when he's trying to look younger and hipper than he is.

'Hi, guys. Would you mind if we had a chat? My name is Simon Ratcliffe. I promote gigs and tours across the North of England through my promotions company. We do most of the big venues. This is my card.'

Stepping forward, he held out his right hand to Dylan.

Despite myself, I felt jealous. Why Dylan? Why not me?

Dylan didn't get up, ignoring the hand that was offered. In fact he slumped back, the euphoria and energy of the performance and our excitement afterwards seeming to leave his body. Simon placed his card on the chair next to Dylan.

'Sure. What can we do for you?' I stepped forward. We had a major promoter wanting to talk to us and Dylan was being rude. Sometimes he was such a loser.

Simon shook my hand and then Andy's. Dylan picked up the card, studying it intently.

'It's good to meet you all. I've heard a lot about you from all sorts of places and tonight I saw for myself: you've got a great sound and the kids love your stuff. I understand you manage yourselves?'

I nodded. 'Yeah, we do all our own organisation. Website and everything.'

'That's great. And have you any plans for the autumn?'

Simon was smooth, but he didn't come across like some kind of music biz shark. At least he was our side of thirty and it sounded like he genuinely liked the music.

I jumped in before Dylan could ruin anything.

'No. We're just trying . . .' I paused, catching myself saying something too true. We needed to look cool, not needy, interested but not sad. 'Well, I mean, we've got recording and stuff and we're doing a few gigs round Leeds, but nothing major. We're working full-time on the band for a year now. Why?'

I got the sense that Dylan had shot me a warning glance but decided not to look.

'Well, I have a regional tour coming up for one of my bigger acts. I'm looking for a support to take on the opening slot. Ten dates across the North, including Liverpool, Sheffield, Manchester and, of course, Leeds. At the Powerhouse.'

It was the biggest venue in the city. I'd seen Coldplay there with my dad when I was little. Coldplay? Oh my God, how embarrassing. But it was a huge place, bigger than anywhere we'd ever played before.

Dylan stared at the ground in silence, like a deflated balloon, so different from just a few minutes before. Andy was looking from me to Dylan and back, as if he didn't know who or how to choose between us.

All I could see were opportunities: if BlackStar could get on a major tour, I would have to choose between that and the *Pop World* gig, if that ever actually happened. If . . . still, that wasn't a bad choice to have for a girl just out of school and trying to get somewhere in the business. It would be one hell of a difficult choice if it ever came down to it.

'Who's the "act" we'd support, then?' Dylan did his best sulking teenager. I was a bit embarrassed.

'Urban Danser,' Simon replied.

I turned back to face him.

'The ones with that song about wine spritzers?' I asked.

It had been on the radio all summer long, driving everyone mad, me especially. It was their second hit. It had a good beat but really stupid lyrics and it was way too poppy, not really our kind of thing.

'The very same. They're playing sell-outs everywhere they go at the moment. I really think you'd complement their style, and it would give you a great platform to build on when you get yourself a deal and start releasing material.'

My heart lurched for a minute. Here was a big-time promoter assuming we were going to get a record deal. This was exciting. I sensed that Simon knew he'd got my attention at least, but he was too canny to think that Dylan could be persuaded tonight, with the mood he was now in.

60

'It's a great opportunity, guys, and I'd love to have you on board. But right now I can see you need some time to think. I'll leave the offer on the table. Have a little talk amongst yourselves and we can discuss details later. An expression of interest at this stage would be really helpful.'

Simon offered his statement as a kind of question. I didn't know what to say. I couldn't speak for everybody. I knew only one person could do that, although I wasn't sure I wanted to hear what he had to say.

Dylan looked up into the lights above the backstage area, rotating the business card in his fingers, and spoke without any hint of emotion.

'Yeah, we've got your number. We'll be in touch. Thanks for the offer.'

With that, he stood up and walked out of the circle of light into the darkness around us.

13

The argument went on for two days. One minute we were doing it, the next it was the last thing on earth that Dylan would ever consider. He was totally against it from the start, but we were a band, and we all had some say in this, so it was never going to be just a straight 'no'.

Early evening, we met up at mine to work on some rhythms on the computer for a new song we were putting together. I never even got to turn it on. I was too frustrated to even look at Dylan by then, after all the texts, the calls, the discussions we'd had over the last forty-eight hours. It had been our best night ever as a band, but we'd never had a minute to even enjoy it. Everything felt like it was coming to a head, like I had to let it all out. It was all just driving me so nuts.

'Look, Dyl, I told him we'd call him by tonight. We have to make a decision. This is an amazing opportunity. You know it is. We can take our music to a whole new audience, and get loads of media exposure, get paid and get some experience. I think we have to do it. I don't think we have any choice.'

I was standing in the middle of the room like a barrister making her case in the courtroom, arms flailing around with every new point.

'What are we gonna do? Sit here for the rest of our lives in my bedroom playing at being musicians? For God's sake, Dyl, we don't even have a record out and we've been offered a tour. This is our big chance! My big chance. You could be ruining it for all of us. We might never get another opportunity to do this.'

I was becoming hysterical and starting to feel a bit silly. I wasn't going to persuade anybody of anything if I went on and on at them, rehashing all the old arguments and screeching like a loony. I paused and sat down quickly on my IKEA bouncy chair, my hands placed firmly under my thighs.

'You're just being stubborn, Dylan, you really are.' And then I finally fell silent. The mini-fridge in the corner with my wine gums in it hummed gently.

Andy gave me a little sympathetic half-smile, hiding it from Dylan, just enough to show he understood, even if he didn't entirely support me. It wasn't the first time Andy's weakness had driven me insane, although in the past I'd managed to stop myself from telling him to go screw himself. I glared at him, causing a look of total fear to cross his face, and turned back to Dylan, where this battle was going to be won or lost.

'Sorry,' I continued, much more calmly. 'It's just that I can't stand the idea that we could miss out on this, even though it's not exactly perfect or what we planned.'

I stopped myself. Surely even Dylan would realise I was right?

'Perfect?' Dylan responded from his position flat out on my bed. 'It's not even close to perfect.' He rolled over and propped himself up on my fluffy pink pillows, the ones I'd got from Camden Market last summer. Part of me wanted to laugh, but it really wasn't the best time for that. 'Urban Danser are a bunch of manufactured talentless pop stars who'll be gone in six months after having one more hit that somebody else wrote for them, probably about cheese or hair slides or something. Do we really want to be known for supporting them?'

Andy was straddling my desk chair, leaning towards us over the back with his big bear arms hugging the sides.

This wasn't going the way I'd hoped. I looked at Andy. Maybe he would finally come through for me, finally be a man about it and stand up to Dylan for once?

'I can see what both of you are saying,' he started, 'it goes both ways for me. My main problem is the time off work. If I do this, I'll have to either take all my holidays for the year or just quit.' Andy looked bewildered. I kind of wanted to reach out to him, but at the same time I was ready to punch him. 'But I can't believe we'd be playing at the Powerhouse, and the Riverside in Newcastle. That's mad. I'd love that. That kind of makes me want to do it.'

For a second, I saw it from Andy's point of view. It was harder for him than for any of us. He didn't just have his dreams to consider. He had to figure out how he could afford to live. But if we did this, he wouldn't have to do his stupid job any more, or worry about anything. I scrambled up any sympathy for Andy's situation and focused back on Dylan, who was staring at the ceiling of my bedroom as if it was some magical work of art, or a different solar system.

I resisted the temptation to clench my fists and start waving them around again. It wasn't worth it. I wasn't going to convince Dylan, and he wasn't going to convince me either.

'Look, we've had this same conversation for two days now and we haven't got anywhere. We need to make a decision and phone the guy with a yes or no, because if we don't we could miss out on it anyway just by being late. I think we should just have a vote. It's the only way.'

I'd avoided this for two days, not wanting to force Andy to side with me in front of Dylan, but it looked like I didn't have a choice. I'd been working on Andy day and night since Monday, by text, by blackmail and by all other means necessary, and I was confident I had his vote. Lads are so easy to manipulate when you've got your hand in the right place. He'd obviously had his doubts, but I reckoned I'd persuaded him we should accept the offer.

Dylan nodded his agreement. 'Cool, a vote it is. Let's do it.'

Nobody spoke for a moment, so I decided to look after the formalities.

'Dylan: for or against?'

'Against. Obviously. Doh.' He stuck out his tongue at me.

I pouted at him. He was so annoying sometimes. At least he wasn't drunk tonight.

'OK. Me: for. Obviously.'

I gave him my best defiant 'coming right back at you' face. Which left Andy.

'Andy? For or against?' I leaned back in the springy chair and waited, pleased with how this was going.

Not for the first time in our complicated three-way band and friendship relationship, Andy glanced backwards and forwards between Dylan and me with an expression of confusion. I felt sorry for him, sorry that he had to do this to Dylan, his best friend forever; sorry he had to do it to Dylan in front of me; sorry that he couldn't be a man and do it himself in the first place.

Andy finally locked on to my gaze.

'I'm sorry, Ell. I can't do the tour. Against.'

14

It was two weeks before I spoke to them again.

I hated every minute of it, but I also hated them for letting me down. I'd heard nothing from *Pop World* either. Could things get any worse? The only thing that made it bearable was that my dad was away with work, so I didn't have him on my back as well, about the internship and *Pop World* and anything else that he could think of.

Andy texted me every hour for a week and must have spent a day's wages on a huge bunch of pink and white roses that arrived a couple of days after the decision was made, but I didn't want to see him and I didn't reply. I couldn't believe he'd sided with Dylan about such a massive thing. I hated him for being so weak, for just agreeing with Dylan because he always did. It was so lame. Most of all, I felt like all his loyalty was in the wrong place, that he'd stabbed me in the back just at the moment when I needed him the most.

And then I remembered my secret audition back in June, and I just got upset.

It wasn't supposed to be like this. How could I, Ellie Batchelor, the most in-control and controlling person in the world apart from my dad, actually have reached a point where I had no control over all the most important parts of my whole life?

Jamie and Kate told me that Dylan had started some serious partying, going out most nights to anywhere he could find somebody to share his self-destructive streak. Wherever he went, particularly at Spirit, he was taking anything he could get hold of, living the rock 'n' roll lifestyle he'd always wanted, just without the rock 'n' roll bit now. I knew he'd always smoked dope, but Jamie said that things were starting to get out of hand now. This was something else.

I knew Jamie and Kate were worried and they kept trying to get me to help, but I kept them at arm's length too. I just couldn't face anybody, knowing how complicated the whole mess had become, and how I couldn't do anything to change it for the better. For the first time in my life, I felt helpless.

Somehow, Jamie managed to keep out of the argument and stay friends with us all. You had to admire his diplomatic skills. He would never be without mates, not like me.

The days dragged on endlessly. I wrote some songs on my mum's piano and played and sang some tunes she liked to her, just to keep her smiling as best I could. She wasn't getting any better, and it was just another major thing to worry about on top of everything else.

I played around with the computer, working on beats for a couple of tracks we'd been putting together earlier in the summer, just after V when we'd been at our most inspired ever, but most of the time I just stared off out of my bedroom window into space, through the soft September rain that had started so soon after our festival success in the park. It was hard to take that it could all be over, and so soon after there'd been so much to hope for.

One day when I had nothing better to do, I went on the computer to surf the web for a bit, checking out my Facebook site and generally tidying stuff up. I took a quick look at my Hotmail account to clear out the usual junk that gathered there. I hadn't been on for weeks. I only used Hotmail for buying stuff and registering at sites, so my inbox was stuffed with spam and all sorts of band ads from MySpace.

I was just about to click 'Delete All', when, for some reason I'll never understand, a subject line from out of all the spam and Viagra adverts drew my attention: **'To Ellie: From Becky: URGENT: POP WORLD!!!'** It was from the girl at the V!

I felt sick. The date of the email was ten days ago. And it said urgent. What had I missed? And why hadn't she used my proper email address? I checked three or four times a day at least. And then I remembered: I'd given her my Hotmail address instead, just in case she turned out to be a bit of a freak and started stalking me all over the internet. Sometimes I wished I could be just a bit less controlling.

I double-clicked on the subject line, dreading what I was going to find, good or bad, not getting my hopes up that anything positive could come of this.

Hi Ellie, remember me? We met at the V in the queue for the toilets!

Sorry I didn't get back to you sooner about all this, but Jenny, my contact at Pop World, vanished for a bit while they were working on their cuts. I've worked with them on another programme and that's what they're all like in TV!

Anyway I've had a word and Jen says they're excited about you and you're on the list of 32 that they're going to cut down to 24 in the next couple of weeks.

From what she said, I think you could make it, but she did suggest you send in a video or a track you've done to her ASAP. They've got the usual varied bunch, and there are a couple of girls your age they're considering but they can't take all of you.

I reckon it could make the difference if you sent them your stuff, the way she was talking.

Competition is tough this year, she said.

Anyway, her email is: jen225@saturdaynight productions.co.uk

Just tell her a bit more about your music as well, maybe send her some pics: you've got a great look so if your music is as good you could be in there!

Anyway, remember me when you're famous, I'll be after an interview! Hope it goes well . . .

I stared at the screen in horror. What if I'd missed my chance? There was less than a week left before the final cut was made. Could it get any worse? What if the producer had been expecting something from me and had got pissed off waiting?

I sat for a few moments staring at the screen, unsure how to respond. It was amazing that they might want me, unbelievable that I might miss out.

Then the Batchelor in me kicked in: time to get on with it and make it happen. I opened the My Videos folder, double-clicked my editing software and began the work.

15

A few days later, Jamie called and begged me to come to Spirit. It was late, but it was good to hear his voice.

'You need to get out, Ell,' he pleaded. 'We haven't seen you for weeks. Andy's not here, he's working and Dyl will be busy with the sound desk, so Kate and I will look after you. What do you think?'

I didn't really need much persuading. I'd been locked in the house with Mum for so long that I thought I might go as mad as she was if I didn't do something about it soon. And if I could avoid Dylan and Andy, it would be great to see Jamie and Kate again. So I went.

The club was heaving as usual. It was Thursday night, so all the students were in. For a few moments I thought about what I might have been doing right now, somewhere in Bristol with my new student mates, no worries about loser bandmates, lost chances of stardom, whether or not *Pop World* would ever happen for me.

Then I cleared my head. I couldn't afford to let Dylan see me like this. He'd only tell Andy and then they'd think I wanted to get back with them again.

Jamie and Kate met me outside from the taxi.

'You look great, Ell, really glam. I love your tights.' Kate knew a great pair of tights when she saw them. They were yellow and green circles all the way down. They looked fab under my black tutu-style mini.

'I've missed you so much, you guys. You have no idea. I just couldn't face anybody after what happened though.'

Kate gave me a big hug and pulled me inside the bar. It was heaving. She shouted right in my ear, so loud that I thought it would explode.

'Don't worry, you're here now and Andy's at work so he won't be around tonight anyway. So let's get a big expensive drink.'

We perched on high bar stools like a couple of flamingos with our mouths over cocktail straws, straining to catch up on the news. Jamie disappeared, leaving us to our shouted gossip. It was great to be back with them, even though I couldn't imagine facing Dylan just yet. That would take some time and some alcohol.

'You know, Ell, I think Dyl feels bad about all this. He's been drinking himself stupid since you turned down the offer, taking poppers, all sorts. You should see him tonight. He's out of it.'

Kate did a whirling gesture with her index finger on the side of her head. 'I'm really worried about him. He's talked to Jamie about going to the Limelight and scoring. Jamie's been trying to keep an eye on him but he can't be with Dylan 24/7.'

God, Dylan really was losing it. My heart went cold. The Limelight was well known as a place you avoided unless you really wanted to get out of your face. But then I thought about Dylan's reaction to Andy's vote. His face had been so smug, so triumphant. My head took over.

'I can't feel a lot of sympathy for him right now, Kate. You don't expect me to make the first move, do you, after what he did?'

I slurped a long slug of Sex on the Beach. Kate agreed.

'Well no, course not. He's stopped you from doing the tour and you and Andy aren't doing well. But,' she paused, as if taking a deep breath, 'it's not like what he's done is much worse than you keeping the audition quiet, is it?'

I looked up at Kate's open face. She could be pretty harsh when she wanted to, but I suppose she had a point. I looked away for a second.

'Yeah, maybe,' I hissed. 'But if we'd taken that tour, I wouldn't even be thinking about doing *Pop World*. That's why I was so mad.'

Kate looked beyond me towards the entrance to the club section. She leaned in, trying to make herself heard above the noise of the bar.

'OK, well you need to think about what you're going to say to Dylan, because he's the one that got Jamie to bring you here tonight. He wants to talk, to get the band back on. He's really missing you and BlackStar. I've just seen him at the other door. Looks like he's coming over.'

Dylan had set this up? I couldn't believe it. He must be

really missing me, after all. But a few mumbled words about getting the band back together weren't going to stop the way I felt about him throwing away what might be our best chance of success.

I turned to see Dylan picking his way through the crowd, head down, floppy hair bouncing. What a dufus.

Suddenly I could feel my phone vibrating in my pocket. I looked down at the number. It was withheld. I hated that. I always take those calls, just in case they're important, and they always turn out to be from some double-glazing company.

I jumped up and shouted to Kate. 'Keep him here, I've just got to take this call outside so I can hear.'

And with that, I melted into the crowd.

16

When I got back in, Jamie and Kate were at the bar. Dylan was nowhere to be seen.

'Ell, come to the dressing rooms, we need to be able to hear ourselves. Dyl is in there already. He wants to talk.'

I nodded steadily. Dylan was really trying. I needed to give him a break.

The dressing room behind the stage was pokey and grim. I'd been in there a few times when we played, and the thumping of the music from outside the club was still powerful enough to shake the ceiling plaster. We used to joke about it coming down on us.

Nobody laughed now. Dylan was sitting in the corner with a guitar in his hands, like it was some kind of shield to protect him from whatever was going to happen. He looked kind of pathetic, lost, but he still had something about him, something that still made me feel just a tiny bit protective over him, despite everything.

Kate and I sat down on the tatty old sofa in the corner by the door. Jamie acted as peacemaker.

'Ell, Dyl wants to talk to you, don't you, Dyl?' He

was firm, but still trying to be jokey about it. 'He's got something he wants to say.' Jamie waited expectantly, looking over at Dylan.

Dylan looked up. I could see he was pissed out of his brain, or buzzing on something. His eyes were miles away, but he held my look for once in his life. It was like looking into an empty well, there was no way you'd ever see to the bottom. Maybe there was no bottom.

'Hi, Ell, how you doing?' He tried to smile, but it came out all crooked and lopsided, and his words were a bit slurred.

Part of me wanted to hug him, look after him, but more of me hated him for all of it; for turning down the tour; for never being ready for anything; for always expecting everyone else to organise him; for being in the wrong place at the wrong time; for never wanting to leave his little bubble that he felt so comfortable in now, comfortable enough to mess around with his life and his friends; and most of all I hated him for being in this state, the same state my mum was in, except that she couldn't help it and Dylan had done it all to himself.

'Hi, Dyl. What is it you want to tell me?' I felt myself becoming bigger, as Dylan got smaller.

He dragged himself up and put the guitar to one side, apparently managing to sober up, at least for a second.

'Your mate Simon called yesterday. He's still wants us as support for the Urban Danser tour. Somebody else pulled out on him.' Dylan seemed unsteady on his feet, but he leaned against a wall and regained his composure.

'So what? You're against us making it at all, Dyl, unless it involves sitting in a shit-hole like this taking drugs and not being able to speak properly. What's changed about that?'

Dylan held his hand out, as if to protect himself from my hard words. He seemed to be summoning up some energy from somewhere to speak.

'I've changed my vote, Ell. I'm for.' He took a deep breath. 'So let's get on with this stupid fucking tour and get it over with. Let's get you all that fame you're after. Andy's up for it.' Dylan seemed to sneer a bit when using Andy's name. 'And I've called Simon Ratcliffe back to tell him we're in. Happy now, Ell?'

He sneered again from under his fringe.

I stared at Dylan in disbelief. How could he let himself down like this? How could anybody? I didn't know where to start.

'Well that's great, Dyl,' I said quietly. 'And you know what, yesterday I might have cared. But today, seeing you like this, thinking you can just change your mind and everything will be OK, make huge decisions for all of us, all on your own, well you're wrong.' I paused, shaking my head at Kate and Jamie and then turning back to Dylan. 'I'm sorry, but it's me that won't be able to make it, this time. You can shove your tour up your backside, Dylan, I'm not interested any more. You and Andy are welcome to it.'

I spat out the words with all the anger and frustration of the last two weeks behind them.

Dylan tried to drag himself fully upright to protest but I cut him short.

'Don't bother even arguing about it, Dyl. I've just had a call from *Pop World*, the TV show.' Dylan looked up, confused. 'Yeah that's right, a talent show. Your favourite.' Now it was my time to sneer. 'It's an opportunity I can't turn down, just like the tour was, but this time it's all my decision. I'm gonna do what's best for me like you should've done for all of us two weeks ago, Dylan, if you'd had the guts to actually get out of your own little world and try and make something of yourself.'

Dylan didn't reply. He slumped back against the wall.

'I'm in the last twenty-four of the competition and I'm leaving for London on Saturday. If I get to the last sixteen I'll be on the first show the week after. The band's over, Dylan. And you can tell Andy that me and him are over too.'

Jamie tried to speak.

'Ell, can't we—'

'No, J.' I stopped him. 'We can't. It's over.'

I stood up and hauled the heavy wooden door open, and left without looking back.

17

Jamie X's BlackStar Blog
24 September 2008 - BlackStar Update
We've been away for a little bit and things have been kind of tough round here for a while, but it's time to let everybody know what's been happening. There's been a load of rumours about Ellie leaving, which she has, but the fans deserve an explanation, after all those adds we've had, and all the brilliant messages of support ever since Daylight Robbery in August.

So it's true: Ellie, Andy and Dylan have split and gone their separate ways, but we're not crying here. We think it's going to turn out great for everybody. Ellie's gone on to do something really special that she's keeping secret just for now and

80

Andy and Dyl told me last night that they wish her good luck in whatever she does. I'm going to be keeping everybody up to date at her site too, so Elliefans can get their fix over there from now on, not here. See her there at www.myspace.com/batchelorpad.

Over here you'll continue to get your samples, links, downloads and updates on everything BlackStar in the known universe, just like you always have. Don't say I don't give you everything that you want! And whatever you do, don't forget the tour dates posted above: including Manchester in two weeks, and the big one in Leeds just before Christmas.

Meanwhile, the boys are thinking they might get a new singer, just maybe, if Dyl can't reach the high notes, obviously. Contact them on our link below, if you think you've got what it takes. Might be useful if you live near Leeds though and have plenty of time to kill!!

18

Boot Camp was fantastic. It lasted for ten days, and all I did was sing and dance and take advice about how to get better.

As well as getting through to the last sixteen.

Obviously.

When I say all I did was sing and dance, that's not strictly true. There was a lot of other stuff going on there that was pretty funny too. Most of it involved this total set of losers who didn't seem to realise that this was the greatest chance they were ever gonna get to be a star, so they spent the whole time throwing it all away. They had talent too, but they just didn't have the commitment, so eight of them went and then we were down to the last sixteen, the ones that really mattered.

On the first day the lads and the girls were separated into two different (very cheap) hotels just up the road from each other and the Boot Camp venue at a theatre in a place called Barking in Essex. There wasn't much to do after the shows. We didn't finish working until after ten, so most of us who were serious about it all went off to bed or had a couple of quiet drinks in the pub next to our hotel. There were some fab people at Boot Camp, but some real tossers too.

One morning early on, before the cut, I linked up for breakfast with Jayani, this really nice girl from Hounslow who sang great R 'n' B. We'd kind of made friends early, sensing we weren't bogus, unlike most of the clones there. Even though both of us realised that the other was likely to be her main competition, we'd managed to set up our own little exclusive support network that had carried us through the vocal coaching, choreography workshops, wardrobe tasks and make-up and hair sessions. I felt like she was one of the first people I'd ever known who was actually like me. She flopped down next to me, furtively holding a copy of the *Daily News*, and grabbed a slice of toast.

'You will never guess what's in here today, Ell,' she whispered behind her hand, mouth full of crumbs, eyes wide open. She nodded with her head at a stick-thin girl who was having her breakfast (her daily glass of water) in a haze of cheap perfume and hairspray, over-made-up as usual and as friendly as ever; i.e. not even a bit.

'Roxy's all over page five. What a dirty slapper! You should see what she's been up to with Gaz/Baz/Daz from Rochdale. Look.'

She opened out the paper on her lap so I could take a peek.

It was hilarious. Jayani and I had given Gaz/Baz/Daz his name after he'd seemed to forget most of the lyrics during his stunning Lancashire accent reggae version of 'Unchained Melody' at last week's first cut. We'd decided that he would probably forget his own name, which was actually Wayne, if somebody asked him what it was. He didn't make it through to the last sixteen in the end, but his tribute name will live on forever in my mind. Bless.

The picture was priceless: Gaz/Baz/Daz climbing out of a hotel window, one leg hanging off the windowsill, a look of pure terror on his bright white face that was fully lit up by flash, framing him perfectly. Maybe he looked so scared because he was only wearing a pair of very girlie bikini bottoms and they seemed to manage to cover up anything 'important' just a bit too easily. Or it might have been because of the prickly bushes he was about to fall into. Either way, it was great.

'Oh my God!' I scanned the rest of the shots. 'Look at this one of Roxy. I didn't realise you could get nighties that were only made of bits of string.'

Jayani did a giggly sort of snort, muffling it with her hands as she tried to cover up her amusement. Her dark wavy hair, perfect as ever when she was in public, fell down over deep, warm brown eyes.

Sweeping it back, she laughed. 'At least she's getting better at something by the looks of it. This place ain't gonna be able to do much for her singing, if you ask me.'

Jayani fixed me with one of her 'talk to the hand, girlfriend' looks that cracked me up. She always slipped into the Diva role when she was having a laugh. She talked in a mix of London/Asian slang and took the piss out of me, and anyone else, for coming from 'oop North'.

'Well, she got into the last twenty-four, so they must think she's got something. She's such a toothpick. I think she only got in so that Martin Harman'll have somebody to pick bits of flesh out of his teeth with after the show's finished. He's freaky, man, I tell you he's always leering at me from the judges' box. Eww.'

I was seriously weirded out by Martin, TV's so-called Mr Music, at times. He was the main judge, but it wasn't that he scared me by his comments, they'd always been really helpful and complimentary. It was more the way that his eyes seemed to wander around below my face when he was talking to me backstage.

Once I realised what he was doing, which part of me his eyes were focusing on, I made sure I always wore a low-cut top from that point on.

That had been over a week ago, but it seemed like years. Now the competition was down to the last sixteen, and everybody knew that it was 'game on'. Jayani and I were in my room, finishing our make-up and hair ready for another day of hard work and practice for the first real show on Saturday night.

It was good having her around. I couldn't trust her, not yet, couldn't trust anyone, but at least it meant I had somebody to talk to, somebody who understood what I was going through and what it had taken to get here. Well, some of what it had taken.

Losing Andy and Dyl had been hard, even though I'd been as angry as hell with them. They'd been my closest friends, my musical partners, and Andy was my rock. It took walking out to realise how much I missed them. Missed them or needed them? Sometimes I wondered, but things were going too well for me at the moment to seriously consider that BlackStar could have been a better choice.

I put that thought out of my mind and linked arms with Jayani as we left the room to take the lift down to the cars that waited to take us to rehearsals every morning, feeling every inch the pop stars that we hoped we'd become soon.

'What are you singing for the first show then?' she said. 'I'm so excited I can't wait. I can't believe I'm gonna be on TV on Saturday!' Jayani was as focused as me. Our conversations always quickly came back to the competition after minor distractions like Gaz/Baz/Daz's pants or Martin Harman's perving.

'I'm thinking of doing one of my own songs,' I said thoughtfully. 'I've been talking with the vocal guy about it and he likes it, so I'm gonna get some more coaching with the backing tracks this afternoon and see. I've been singing it for ages so at least I feel comfortable with it.'

'Yeah,' said Jayani, 'I think it's best to do something you know and love. I'm gonna do a Rihanna song, one of her early ones. Some people will know it, but it won't be just another bad version of "Ain't No Sunshine" or whatever the wannabees always do.' In one of our bitchy moments, Jayani and I had decided the rest of the competition had no chance. But even when we were being serious, we'd decided both of us had a great chance of winning.

We stepped out of the lift to see our fellow contestants, the wannabees themselves, all sitting around not talking to each other, staring intently into pocket mirrors, adding liquid, powder or gloss to various parts of their bodies as they waited for their cars in the hotel foyer. They all looked like bad versions of people who were already famous. There was a J-Lo in the corner, a Posh Spice on the sofa. Over by the revolving door there was a Lemar, bobbing his head to his iPod and humming out loud whilst smoothing back his tight cornrows. Jayani turned and laughed.

'See. Some of them are even wannabees of wannabees!'

At least Jayani understood that it had to be about the music, like me. I thought about my song for the weekend: 'Love Life Message'. It had been the most downloaded of all BlackStar's songs from our website and got the best reaction whenever we did it live. People had been shouting for it at the Daylight Robbery gig. It was a great song, really soulful but with modern beats, a ballad but not one of those sad ones, something a bit special. Something real. Everybody always said so.

I'd been singing it for ever, perfecting the tone, the style, loving every minute of singing the song that was going to make me a star. Dylan always loved the way I did it too. It was one of the few things he used to get excited about. He used to say nobody could ever do it better, that I'd made the song mine, every single time I sang it.

It's true, I had made 'Love Life Message' mine, almost as soon as Dylan had written it.

19

The night before the first show, Jamie emailed me and I picked it up on my new BlackBerry. My dad had bought me it for getting into the last sixteen and it meant I could get my emails and calls wherever I was, as long as they had WiFi. Obviously, everywhere I went because of *Pop World* in London had it, so I was sorted.

Jamie wasn't trying to piss me off, he's just not like that, but he did. His email was full of news about home, stuff that I wanted to know about, but some of it could have waited for another couple of days.

From: jmeex@hotmail.com
To: lilacswirlzagain@aol.com

Hi Ell how u doing? ☺
Just a quickie to say good luck and hope you're ready for the show tomorrow, everybody here is talking about it. The whole city's going Elliemad. Lol. You're a star and you haven't even started yet. I did an article about you in the Mercury so I've

attached it for you to look at. Bet you've been a bit busy to check out the Yorkshire press recently he he.

Kate and I'll be watching on TV. Next time I want an invitation at least. I know you said you didn't want anyone there for the first one but hey, I wanna get my haircut on national TV just as much as you do x Dylan and Andy are gonna be watching too, even though they both said they'd rather eat their own vomit. I didn't believe them. Dylan had his shades on when he said it . . . always a giveaway. (Sorry . . . thought you'd like to know x x I'm sure they'll get over it.)

Anywayz, so what's happening here? Well Kate's got a new boyf, sure she's told you already, but he's a knob so I thought I'd let you know before you decided he was OK. He's called Jonathon . . . sad but loaded. She'll get over it soon. There's been a couple of great gigs at Spirit, Holy Molly were on again. They've got a deal with RPA and they're going on tour with the Chiefs next January.

Me and Kate saw Jessica Lewis and that Emily girl who used to give you shit at school yesterday in town. You're gonna love this: they were at the Italian on Boar Lane and were going on about their gap years and how they're gonna do a tour of spas in southern Europe or some crap like that, so I mentioned you were gonna be on Pop World on Saturday. You should've seen their faces. They'd obviously heard, but they couldn't help it: Emily went bright red and fished in her bag for something and Jessica just ignored me and pretended I hadn't spoken. LOLOLOL. Love it. BlackStar's tour started last week and it's going all right ☺. Went to the first 2 gigs in Sheffield and Hull and they were good. Loads of tweenagers pissed on cider dancing badly to Urban Danser but we sold quite a lot of T-shirts and there's been a lot more interest on the website. I think they all love Dylan's voice. OK the girls all love HIM really, but the singing is OK too, just not you. It lets them down a bit, but hey they still sound great overall. They've got some new stuff which is excellent . . . you'd love it.

Anyway, I just wanted to wish you good luck and fill you in on everything going on back here. Not much else to say. I've got a gig at Spirit tonight . . . I'll say hi from you and maybe put a few of those sound clips of you in the mix . . . deffo when you're famous!!!

Love u ☺

J xx x

I read it in my dressing room at the TV studio just before final rehearsals. I was so glad BlackStar were doing well without me. Not. But at least I was making a bit of a stir back home too. It wasn't like I felt threatened by the lads and what they were doing; it just put a bit more pressure on me to do better. Which I obviously would.

I went out on stage and nailed it on my final rehearsal. The lights were hot and blinding, but behind them I could see the judges and the cameras all looking directly at me. It was how I'd always imagined fame would be. Leeds felt like it was a million miles away and Jamie's email had only made me better. That was the difference between me and BlackStar: what I wanted, I went and got. They just hung around waiting for it all to happen to them.

20

The next day was like a dream. It passed so quickly that it's hard to even remember any details about what happened.

We were carted out of the hotel at seven in the morning by a bunch of helpers, through a crowd of photographers at the front of the TV studios, and into a huge open area where we had to do interviews for three hours with the press. It was so that the press had their background stories long before the vote was over on Saturday night around ten. That way, they could write their pieces before the show even started and just choose which ones to run as soon as the vote was in and they knew who had been kicked out.

My interviews lasted the longest and I was still there with a few journalists after everybody else had been taken back to the dressing-room area, which was a bit weird. They seemed to be really interested in me, though, so I did my best to be the star I wanted to be and act professional. They asked me about my life in Leeds and my childhood, and even about my family. It was all pretty easy to manage.

I kept up my excitement levels throughout, as I'd been instructed to do by the production team, even when I was explaining about the song I was doing tonight. It had been decided that I would sing a cover version of the Dolly Parton and Whitney Houston classic 'I Will Always Love You'. The producers had decided against me doing 'Love Life Message', feeling that it would be 'too demanding' for viewers on my first appearance. I'd reluctantly agreed after quite a few 'discussions' where I had managed to give my opinion without shouting or losing my temper, but in the interviews I gave the impression that it was the greatest idea since kiss-proof lipstick.

After lunch, we were in make-up, hair and costume for hours and hours until it was time for the show to go out live at six-thirty. Jayani and I had time to sneak a couple of minutes in my dressing room before we were separated out for the night into different areas. We weren't allowed to see each other again until everybody had performed.

'Good luck, babe,' she whispered, scared we'd be discovered and sacked for having friendly conversations without the permission of our 'handlers', as our personal assistants were politely called by the production staff. Ours had been called to a last-minute meeting. They would be back any minute to lock us away again.

'You too.' I hugged Jayani tightly. It had been great having her there. I genuinely wanted her to do well. Just not as well as me.

'Whatever happens, you and me are tight, OK?' she breathed into my shoulder, both of us trying to avoid smudging make-up or tangling our big tousled hair. The dressing room smelled of perfume and make-up, a heavy, thick scent that made me feel slightly nauseous.

'No worries. Tight as a donkey's ass,' I joked as we separated. Jayani laughed.

'You northerners are freaks, you know that?'

'Yeah well, just get used to it, we've got weeks of this still to go.'

I planned to be here for a long time, and I knew she would be too.

'OK, Ell, you'll nail it. We're the best here. Go for it . . .'

Jayani squeezed my hand as Sandra, my handler, opened the door and frowned. She was like my old French teacher, wiry, grey-haired, but obviously clued up. In no time at all, Jayani was gone and Sandra was outside my door on her stool, firmly guarding my privacy. I was due on in eighteen minutes, and in my room I got on with my vocal exercises and checked out my lyrics on the word sheets, praying I didn't forget them and turn into Gaz/Baz/Daz in front of more than ten million people.

Sixteen minutes later Sandra led me down to the wings, where I listened, excited, terrified, disbelieving, as I was introduced.

'And now, from Leeds, singing "I Will Always Love You", it's Elliana Batchelor!'

The music started to twinkle and grow around me as I walked out on stage, the lights rising as I made my way down the central stairway on to the podium where my mark was hidden from the audience by the clever sloping stage. I reached the microphone in time to compose myself and sing the first line of the song.

Five minutes later I was back in my dressing room.

I clicked my BlackBerry back from standby and it lit up with text messages. There were six on the list, including Kate, Dad and Jamie.

And one from Dylan's number. It was the first time I'd heard from him in a month. I opened it up.

```
What a performance Ell. You sounded just
like all the others. And in a shiny old-
woman dress with pearls and a fake tiara
too. Hope you think it was all worth it.
Dylan x
```

I sat and stared at my dressing-table mirror, trying to take it in.

Dylan was so classy, so thoughtful.

What a bastard.

21

I got through the first show, not brilliantly, but OK. The producers gave us all individual feedback on the Sunday, and they told me I'd come tenth out of the sixteen. Jayani came top. She deserved it though. I saw her performance on my dressing-room TV and she really was amazing. I knew I had a lot of work to do.

My dad came to visit me on my day off on the Monday, and took me out for lunch. It was good to get away from all the intense pressure to 'do the right thing' all the time, because everybody on the show was watching and judging you, not just on your performances either.

We settled into a little Moroccan place on the King's Road, a place where my dad always took his clients when he was in London for meetings. It was lovely, totally anonymous, and it felt good to know that things were working out for me, to some extent at least.

'So what sort of feedback have you had from your coaches and the judges then?' Dad asked after we'd ordered and I'd started slurping on an Apple and Mango J2O. He loved it when I ordered non-alcoholic drinks.

He felt he was a good father then.

'Oh you know, the usual stuff. I need to be more dynamic with the vocal changes, awareness of eye contact with the judges, general stuff about my image. After what Martin said on Saturday about me looking like I'd been working Vegas for twenty years, I'm having a makeover for next week's show.'

Dad took a swig on his whisky and Coke.

'Yes, you need to get that sorted out. I don't know what they thought they were doing getting you to sing something so unsuitable for you. You did a decent job, but it's just not you. I suppose they'll be trying to refocus you towards the teen market this week?'

His eyebrow twitched upwards as it always did when he was asking a question that was really an instruction. I let it sit there for a few seconds. Eventually it came back to rest on top of his eye.

'Yep, I've got some ideas for a song that would suit me better.' I didn't want to tell him it was an old BlackStar track. He'd never seen the band anyway, so mentioning 'Love Life Message' would have been a complete waste of time. 'I'm going to give a few of my own ideas this week . . . you know me, can't keep my mouth shut for too long before I make a few changes.'

We both smiled. It was great to be with my dad when he was relaxed and not too pushy. Unfortunately, those times didn't last for long. Today was no exception. The waiter finished placing our food in front of us and then left us alone. Dad leaned in to me.

'I'm glad we've got a chance to talk properly,' he started, picking up his fork in his right hand, leaving the knife untouched. 'I'm sure this is going to be a successful venture for you, as long as you stick to the way we've always done things.' He paused, taking a small piece of chicken into his mouth, his eyebrow heading north again.

I thought about 'the way we'd always done things' for a moment. I couldn't remember us having some amazing plan, or my dad having done something spectacular to make me into a winner. He thought that constantly telling me to want something more than anyone else was the key to it, driving home to me that I should be practising instead of making friends, rehearsing moves instead of watching the TV or playing a computer game. In my own mind, I just thought I'd won because I'd been better than everybody else.

'It's the Batchelor way, Ellie, don't forget. You need to focus on the prize and then do anything you need to do to win. Remember the nationals for Dance Unsigned? I got you the videos for all your main rivals so you could study them and outperform them all. That's what I call commitment.'

Dad reached across the table and grasped my hand.

'Yeah, I was five at the time, Dad. How could I forget? Half those girls never spoke to me again when I fessed up to Jenna Robinson in the dressing room full of their mums after I'd collected the trophy.'

It was ironic really. I'd been sent to Coventry by twenty-five pre-schoolers for admitting to watching their performances so I could beat them. In fact, I hadn't had a proper look at the tapes, just a few minutes to make myself feel better that I could beat them. I'd pretended I'd done it properly to Mum, who told Dad I had when he got home late in the evening from wherever he used to go every night after work at that time. And I'd only admitted it to Jenna because I thought she'd be my friend if I gave her tips on how she could improve.

'Well, it was worth it in the end. You wouldn't be here today if it wasn't for all that work and focus when you were little. I really want you to get this, so make sure you pull out all the stops this week, and every week, OK?' The eyebrow shot upwards, almost apologetically this time, and I could tell that my dad felt helpless for once in his life, unable to help me, or to think he was helping me, whichever helped him the most.

'Don't worry, Dad, I've got it covered.' I nibbled on some really tasty couscous, flavoured with spices and roasted vegetables, and decided to change the subject. There was only so much parental pressure I could take these days. 'How's it going at work? Did they get somebody else to do my intern job?'

'No, no. There was no need. It was a created job anyway, and they'll be happy whatever happens. Things are going well. I've got a new account with NT Petroleum. They have offices all over the world.' I smiled at him. He was the only person I'd ever seen who could get excited about work. Apart from Dylan, although his work was my excitement too.

'Cool. Sounds like you're going to be busy.'

'Yes I am, and that's something I need to talk to you about too.' He put down his fork and folded his napkin across his lap. 'I can't keep waiting for your mother to deal with the legal matters that still need tying up. The last time I went there she was practically comatose, she'd had so many of those bloody tranquillisers she's on, or whatever they are.'

'What?' I said, shocked. 'What do you mean, comatose? What happened?' I suddenly didn't feel very hungry any more.

'Just what I said. I went to the house and it took forty minutes to get her to answer the door. When I did, she was in her nightie, slurring her words.' I gave him a questioning look.

'Is she OK, Dad? You're really worrying me.'

'Look she's fine, it was just the usual stuff. A way of drawing attention to herself and making out like everything is everybody else's fault. I'm afraid it's just not my problem, Ellie.'

I stared into my dad's heavy, reddening face. He looked like an alcoholic sometimes, not surprising when you saw how much he drank. In fact he probably was an alcoholic, even if he didn't know it or care. I tried to find some words to challenge him, make him face up to his part in what had happened to my mum, make him see sense, but as ever, they wouldn't come. He was the only person in the world I couldn't stand up to.

'All I want to do is to get all the paperwork signed off and then it's finished and we can all move on. In time, you'll see it was all for the best, darling.'

Again he started to reach across the table to grasp my hand, as if that would somehow make him seem more human. This time, I quickly placed it under the tablecloth out of reach. Not for the first time, I realised how little my dad cared about anybody other than himself, even if he pretended otherwise.

'Can we go now? I've got to get on with some rehearsing back at the hotel.'

I looked up into my dad's empty eyes. There was no love, no compassion. Perhaps there had been once, but it was all eaten up now by bitterness and a competitive instinct that trampled over anybody that got in its way. I wondered how much like my dad I was. And then I dismissed the thought immediately. It was too much to even consider, right now.

Dad hadn't come here to help me or support me, just as for all those years he hadn't really supported me in my dancing and singing competitions or my schoolwork. It was all about him and what reflected glory he could get from having 'the most talented daughter', or 'the brightest student in the class'. Now he was here to pressurise me into winning *Pop World* just for him too.

'Course we can. I have a meeting in the City in an hour too. I was just going to get the bill anyway.' He looked at me quizzically, as if trying to work out if something was wrong. How could he not see?

'Don't forget, give it everything this week. And if you see any weaknesses, particularly in that Asian girl everyone's talking about, exploit them. You're not some second-rate, washed-up Whitney Houston; you're going to be a star. My star. Remember that.'

With that he stood up and strode over to the waiter, talking furtively, probably negotiating a deal about the size of the tip he was going to leave.

22

Daily News: 3 October 2008

Motormouth Girls Gossip Column

POP WORLD WAR?

How about a little bit on the side?

We're committed to bringing you all the news and goss on this year's fab sixteen contestants on *Pop World*, where amazing R 'n' B diva, Jayani, is making the early running.

Hot on her diamante-studded heels on Saturday night were the Bolton Brothers, from, er, Bolton, and Johnny Spillane, the 70-year-old Sinatra-style crooner from Southgate, London.

Meanwhile, we're hearing an interesting snippet from the Ellie Batchelor camp. The girl's got talent, but she took quite a battering from Martin Harman's wicked whinging tongue last week, forcing her to rethink her image and take stock of where she's going to be on Saturday night.

And now it seems this girl has a history, and it's catching up with her, almost literally. As the Ex lead singer of the newest up-and-coming unsigned band from Leeds, BlackStar, Ellie thought she'd made a step up from the indie circuit to real stardom at *Pop World*.

But maybe her former band is going to catch her on the way up? Or back down?

All the rave reviews in the music press of their latest tour suggest that BlackStar could soon be giving young Ellie a run for her money . . . apparently they're stealing the show every night from Urban Danser, the current number one pop sensations, a band that they're only supposed to be supporting.

Sounds to us like the tail wagging the dog. Let's hope for her sake that Ellie can rise to the challenge too. Could be an interesting pop war on the horizon for the rest of us!

23

The second week flew by after my day-off meeting with Dad. I worked my ass off all week, picking up my vocal routines with the coach and doing extra sessions, meeting with my stylist to give her my own ideas, and doing loads of cardio-vascular stuff to make sure I was ready physically for the challenges ahead. All that stuff also helped me forget what was going on at home with my mum.

Call me a bitch, but I hadn't phoned home for a week, and it had been hard not to call right after I'd seen Dad, but I knew I needed to focus myself on me for a while now, if I was going to have any chance at all of winning this thing, without all the added pressures that calling home might bring.

Jayani was with me like my shadow during that week, matching me meeting for meeting, session for session with the coaches. It started to irritate me a bit, the way I would tell her my next move, such as a visit to the gym, only to find she'd copied it a couple of hours later. She was my competition, but I thought she was my friend too. I knew I would need to think carefully about how to play things with her.

Late on Thursday, after dinner when nobody, not even Jayani and I, spoke to one another, I decided I needed the comfort of a friendly voice that couldn't possibly make me feel worse, only better, so I went straight to my room to give Kate a call. We'd got into the habit of texting a couple of times a day when my schedule allowed me to even look at my phone, but I hadn't had a proper chance to talk to her for ages. Once we'd caught up with how everybody was dealing with my new fame up in Leeds and how she'd dumped Jonathon because he had a sweat problem, as well as a personality defect that involved believing he was Justin Timberlake's English look-alike-ee, complete with little black hat, we got on to more important matters.

'Come on then, what's Jermaine really like?' She laughed. 'He's well fit, his body is gorge. Have you been getting to know him a bit then?'

She giggled as I snorted. 'God, Kate, your taste gets worse. He's the biggest big-headed big-head I've ever met. All he does is oil his big-head hair and look in his compact mirror to check he's still lovely enough. And his voice isn't bad, but he's got no emotion in it at all, has he?'

'Ellie, get over yourself. I know emotion in a voice is important to you, but I really couldn't give a toss about it. All I know is that he's a fine-looking man. And if we're talking big heads, you know what the papers are saying about his tight trousers. God it's huge. Anyway, I'm still voting for you, but if you lose I'll switch . . .'

I sensed that for a split second Kate was unsure how I'd take her joke.

'Oh I see,' I wound her up, 'it's like that, is it? Well you can just vote for him and his massive head now if you like. After this weekend I won't need your vote anyway, everything's changing from now on.'

She giggled. 'OK then, I believe you. You sound confident. The other day when you texted me it sounded like the end of the world. What's happened?'

'I guess I've just started to focus on me and what I need to do. So much has gone wrong over the last couple of months, and if I'm gonna win this thing I'm going to have to zone out all the crap and concentrate. I've taken control of Saturday a bit more. You're going to love it, trust me.'

Kate sounded intrigued.

'Why, what are you doing?'

'Can't tell you just yet. It's all a big secret. Just make sure you're watching. It'll be fab, I promise.'

Kate laughed again. 'I'll bet. When you're in this mood, Ell, nobody's gonna beat you. I know you too well.'

I heard a noise in the background and Kate's hand pressed over the phone to muffle her voice.

'Kate?' I said. I couldn't make out what was being said, but a conversation was going on.

'Sorry, Ell. Just a sec.'

A few moments later she was back.

'Hi, sorry about that. It's just that Andy's here. I said he should speak to you, if you want to. Do you? I know you haven't talked for ages, but it's about time you did.'

For a moment I was unable to reply. I thought about how betrayed I'd been when he had voted with Dylan against the tour, and all those months when being with Andy had been more of a job than a pleasure. Then I looked around the walls of my hotel room and realised I wouldn't be here if I hadn't betrayed him a bit too. And he'd been my rock when everything had been wrong before. And I could do with another comforting, supportive voice right now . . .

'Does he want to? I will if he does . . .' I said, quietly, hoping that this wasn't a set-up and Andy wouldn't just throw it back in my face now.

'Yeah, he's here, just a sec . . .'

I heard the crackles of the exchanges of the phone from Kate to Andy, and then that familiar, deep and warm voice of his, almost wrapping me up like a chocolate blanket. I'd missed him so much, both of them.

'Hi, Ell, how are you doing?' he said.

I tried to hold back the tears that were threatening to come. What was wrong with me? I'd taken control these last few days. Now I was about to lose it again.

'I'm OK. How are you? I heard the band was doing well?' I mumbled, just to say something.

'Yeah,' he said slowly, always Andy, always honest and reliable and kind and generous, despite everything, 'it's not bad. The tour is OK, but you're doing better. You're getting loads of press up here. And you don't have to hear

Urban Danser's set every night for one thing. That's got to be a bonus.'

I giggled. 'Yeah, there is that. But I'm surrounded by a bunch of wannabees singing Michael Macdonald covers here. Not much in it, is there?'

I could tell Andy was smiling, I knew him so well. Even though there was no sound at the other end of the phone I could imagine his big wide smile and sticky-outy cute lips. He never made his feelings very obvious, especially not on the phone, but right now I knew him completely.

I thought quickly. I'd love to tell him all about the show on Saturday, let him know my big news. I'd been dying to share it with somebody. But how would he react? Maybe he wouldn't like the idea and then this lovely, normal, friendly, kind conversation that I'd craved for weeks would come to an end before it had even properly started.

In a split second I made the decision to keep the secret. No point in spoiling things now: I needed the support that Andy was giving me just by agreeing to talk. I couldn't bear to lose it.

'Nothing's worse than Urban Danser, Ell, trust me. They have six costume changes in eight songs and most of them are made of cardboard and bits of wire. They do my head in. Anyway, what's it like with all the attention down there then? Bet you love it, don't you?'

We carried on talking for a while about nothing in particular, which was just perfect. Hearing his voice was enough and when we finally ran out of things to say because there was so much to say (if you know what I mean) I was glad that we'd talked, glad that we hadn't decided to live in the past, at least.

I put my phone down and lay down on my bed, properly relaxed for the first time in weeks, snuggling into my pillow as I started to turn my mind back to what needed to be done.

In a few seconds I was up on my feet again. I pressed 'Play' on the CD player on my side table and listened. As the first few bars of the *Pop World* version of 'Love Life Message' started to play, I thought about how Dylan and Andy would react to me singing it on Saturday. I couldn't have told Andy. Maybe he would've been fine with the idea, maybe not. I just needed a bit of kindness for a few minutes. Was that too much to ask?

And they'd just have to find out about the song at the same time as everybody else.

24

The DJ pushed a couple of knobs and twisted another and spoke into the big dangling microphone in front of him in a singsong voice, guaranteed to wake up the morning commuters of Britain.

'And that was the new release from the Kaisers. Great song. Sounds like another number one to me. What do you think, guys?' There was the sound of clapping in the background from a small group of people. 'Yep, it's got the Morning Gang seal of approval.'

Steve Carrol clicked the mouse on his computer screen and read from the script in front of him, headed 'Breakfast Drive Show, Wednesday, Steve Carrol and the Morning Gang'.

'So up to the news and sport we have a special True Radio exclusive for you this morning, on your national independent station that stays TRUE to the music. True Radio.'

'Whooo . . . True . . .' The sound came from the four gang members gathered on the other side of the desk. I cringed, looking across at Sandra for support, immediately realising she wasn't going to give me any.

'Yep, she's been the talk of the nation since Saturday night with her stunning performance on *Pop World*, when Martin Harman confirmed what we'd all seen, that a star was born.' There was a pause as some fanfarey-type music sounded in the background, before Carrol carried on. 'Everybody's talking about her, it seems like the whole world wants a piece of her, but today she's only talking to you and me on *Breakfast Drive* on True Radio, 102.5 FM. Guys, give it up for our special guest, Ellie Batchelor!'

A huge swell of applause filled the room as fake audience sounds were played to accompany the clapping of the Morning Gang, lots of whooping and whistling.

'Ellie, so good to see you. How are you doing this morning?'

I leaned in on my microphone and smiled, dropping into the professional style I'd begun to feel was almost second nature. I didn't have any nerves. Saturday night had got rid of them. My time had come and I was ready for this stuff.

'Good, thanks, Steve. What about you?'

'Brilliant, Ellie, just brilliant, and all the better for seeing you in the studio. Beats having to look at their ugly mugs every day.' I expected a gesture towards his crew and some kind of hilarious interaction between them all, but Steve was simply following the script, and kept his eyes glued on the computer screen, while the gang members shouted out their own scripted outrage.

It had been an early start this morning. I was woken at

five by Sandra, and in with the stylists until seven, making sure that I had a little bit of input into what I was going to wear and my hair look for the morning. There were still things I wasn't happy about: I'd never worn red lipstick in my life before, for instance. But I felt comfortable in the studio, enjoying the glow of celebrity at last.

'Ah, they're not that bad really, Steve,' I said, playing along.

'OK, we'll have to agree to differ on that, darling,' he laughed, 'but let's get down to business. Tell all about the last few days. I bet it's been amazing, eh?'

'Yeah, it's all been a bit mad, you know. I mean, after the show on Saturday when we found out the results it was great, but then the papers on Sunday had loads of really nice stuff in them about me and I've done loads of photo-shoots in the last day or two as well. I haven't had a minute to let it all sink in yet.'

I smiled, hoping this was coming across OK.

'Well the world's at your feet now, Ellie. True Radio got thousands of calls after the show asking for us to play your music. And everybody I've spoken to since Saturday night has been talking about your voice and your look, and saying you could be the next Leona or Kelly Clarkson. What do you think about that?' The DJ's voice rose at the end, like he was shouting in excitement instead of a question.

'Erm, it's really flattering to be even talked about and especially when people mention those kind of names, Steve. But, you know what, I want to be known for my own style

113

and my singing, for me. I don't want to copy anybody. Those artists are amazing, don't get me wrong, I just want to make my own way without comparisons.'

'You're already incredibly unique.' Carrol looked up into my eyes for the first time and held my gaze. 'You're beautiful, talented and very special. Everybody can see that.' I realised with a shudder that this forty-five-year-old man was actually coming on to me.

'Oh you're so sweet, Steve. But it's got to be all about the music, I think, not clothes and looks and all the shallower stuff.'

The DJ looked surprised. 'How do you mean?'

I realised he wasn't used to guests who moved off script.

'Well, like the song I did on Saturday was one I've been singing for a long time. I used to do it in a band I was in before. They're called BlackStar. They're really good. The guy who wrote it is called Dylan Patrick. He's incredibly talented, a great guitarist too. It's where I got my start and I really loved my time in the band.'

Carrol's eyes seemed to glaze over for a minute and I realised I needed to keep my answers short: the producers had warned me to be brief when I'd left for the show. Apparently, listeners only had a short attention span.

'I get you, Ellie. I'm sure you did. But hey, it's another world now, isn't it?' Carrol seemed to have got himself back on track. 'You know what, take a look out of the window at the London skyline just now.' He paused for a second, as if gesturing to me. I looked up, a bit surprised, as his eyes remained rooted to the screen. We were in a studio that was completely enclosed by dark walls, about four metres square, max, stuffed with people and equipment. 'Look. Come here,' he continued, as if we were moving. 'Over there's St Paul's, Canary Wharf, see? Oh and see the Tower of London? You know what I'm thinking, Ellie?'

He glanced over at me with a bit of a warning look in his eyes, letting me know I was supposed to speak and keep up the game. I was a bit worried about what I might have to say about the non-existent buildings.

'What are you thinking, Steve?' I purred in my best flirty voice. I'd been told flirting was good, especially if I couldn't think of something to say. Maybe it would distract him.

'I think that one day, all this is going to be yours. First London, then the world.' He laughed out loud at his cheesy words, and the Morning Gang joined in on cue. I chuckled as best I could.

'Aww that's so sweet of you, Steve,' I replied. 'I've got to win first though, remember. Don't forget this is only Week Two of sixteen. I need all the help I can get every week from the public with their votes.'

'No worries, no worries, you can leave that to us,' Steve said. 'You're now True Radio's favourite for this year's *Pop World* and we're supporting you all the way. Vote Ellie. That's what we say. The campaign starts now . . .'

I beamed at him, a genuine smile this time. I'd obviously done OK with the interview.

Carrol moved to turn up the music for the next song. As

he did, he leaned towards me over the mixing desk as the music came up to full volume.

'You know, on a clear day, we can see all the way to Brighton?' he murmured, winking, placing his sweaty fat hand over mine and giving it a squeeze.

I laughed uncomfortably.

He wrote some numbers on a piece of paper and folded it into my hand as the rest of the gang stood up and went about their various studio jobs.

'Call me,' he mumbled, in a mid-Atlantic drawl.

I smiled sweetly, taking the folded piece of paper and carefully stowing it away in my bag, ready to be shredded, burned, spat on and eaten in the car on the way home.

I'd always known I was in a game. I just hadn't known some of the rules. Now I knew a few more.

25

I was all over the papers again the following weekend, and had started to like all the attention. It was strange, Jayani hadn't got this much press after her win in Week One, but the producers kept telling me that Martin Harman's comments had swung it my way after my second show, and that the buzz was growing around me. I just had to ride with it, do what they said, and I would be OK.

The weekend of the third show, I had a double-page centre spread in the *Daily News*. It was all fantastic stuff. I sat in my room, my only private place now, reading over and over all the quotes they'd got from all sorts of people about me: music business people, record producers, DJs and other artists, all really over-the-top, complimentary stuff. I had to pinch myself still to believe it was me they were talking about.

And they'd used Martin's words from the week before as the headline: 'Ellie Batchelor: the future of British pop', it read. Martin had added that he'd never seen such an amazing performance in all his years as a pop Svengali. I'd blushed and held my face in my hands. Alongside the articles, there were some pictures from the photo-shoots I'd done during the week, plus a few of me walking around in London outside various cool and famous places I'd been taken by the production team. I was looking pretty good, I have to say.

On the bottom right-hand side of the page there was an article about Dylan. I read it nervously. What had he said about me now?

Daily News
Saturday

BATCHELOR BOY'S GOT NO STYLE, *MAN*

He was named after a famously angry folk protest singer of the Sixties, and Dylan Patrick, writer of Ellie Batchelor's stunning 'Love Life Message', seems to be a huge chip off that boring old block. And just like Bob himself, this Dylan's got a huge chip on his shoulder as well: except his seems to be about our Ellie, the nation's favourite.

The News caught up with Patrick at a grungy, squalid club in South Leeds last night – hardly the glamorous kind of haunt that Ellie finds herself in these days – where he spilled the beans on the stormy relationship that led to BlackStar, Ellie's former band, splitting up, just before she turned up to wow us on *Pop World*.

Patrick was obviously high on something as he spewed out his spiteful words. 'She's just turning into a manufactured bimbo,' he said of his former friend. 'She had the chance to make it with us, but stabbed us in the back and gave it all up for some stupid game show and now she looks like a sad cow. She's s**t. It's all s**t. We're well f***ing better.' Most of Patrick's comments were unprintable in a family newspaper.

Clearly jealous of Ellie's success on *Pop World*, Patrick refused to comment when asked about Ellie's brilliant performance of his song, 'Love Life Message', on *Pop World* last week. 'As if I'd watch s**t like that,' he sneered.

However later in the evening, slumped practically unconscious under the influence of something in the doorway of a nearby shop (*see picture right*), 'friends' nearby suggested he'd been glued to the TV just like the rest of us that night.

Jamie Sanderson, known locally as 'Jamie

X', had a different take on Dylan's reaction. He claimed: 'Dylan was really pleased for Ellie after we'd all watched *Pop World* together. We had a bit of a party round ours. There's no problem between them.'

It seems that Dylan Patrick might be in denial about the future. His band is causing some concern on the music scene with its hard partying image, even managing to get themselves banned from one venue after an incident between Patrick and Glorious Georgious, the fabulous lead singer of pop sensations Urban Danser.

Patrick declined to comment on the rumours, but Sanderson also denied there had been a falling-out between the two bands on their joint tour. 'It's all just a load of malicious rumours,' he said. 'Dylan loves Urban Danser and him and Glorious will be hanging out again at the next gig. They always have a few beers after the show to wind down. Dylan's getting ready to write his next masterpiece, so he hasn't time for chucking people's space costumes out of windows.'

Whatever the truth of it all (and our sources suggest the problems on the tour

remain unresolved) it seems that Dylan
Patrick isn't going to be able to compete
with Ellie Batchelor and the start of her
trip to superstardom.

One tip, Dylan: get yourself a stylist;
lying in your own vomit in a stained old
army jacket isn't gonna win you admirers
any time soon . . .

I felt a bit sick as I was reading it. Next to all those lovely
pictures and articles about me, he had to come out and say
all those horrible things, he couldn't just be happy for me.
And all because I'd got there first and BlackStar were still
pretty much nobodies. I'd only told people that he'd written
the song so that he could maybe get some benefit for
BlackStar out of it and he'd thrown it back in my face in the
national papers.

And what the hell was he doing sitting in Superdrug's
doorway looking like a tramp? It was a blurry picture, but it
made me think of those people you see late at night when
you're coming home from clubbing: the ones with nowhere
to go, nobody to care for them.

OK, sure, maybe he was having a bad time, but when
I thought about it, whose fault was that? It's not like he
didn't have the chance to do the tour with me in the band.
He was the one who couldn't make up his mind and
who was too 'cool' to tour when I wanted to. And where
would BlackStar be now if that had happened? In a better

place than Dylan seemed to be, that's for sure.

I pulled out the middle pages and folded it carefully into my newly-formed Ellie Scrapbook, where I kept all the exciting things that were starting to accumulate in my room. It was just one of those folding boxes from Birthdays, but it was important to me to keep it all together. I knew I'd only just begun, though; there would be plenty more stuff to put in my scrapbooks in the future.

And Dylan could stick it. If I'd still had any feelings for him before, they were gone now. It was time to get on with the show.

26

Weeks flew by as the competition got more and more intense. It seemed more like just a few days had passed, not a couple of months, before we were down to the last six: the Bolton Brothers, Jayani, me, Jermaine, Vickee, the blind girl from Scotland and a group of black soul brothers called Oxygenes.

I knew I had a great chance. Although I hadn't had the same kind of brilliant voting figures ever since the second show, I was still always in the top three or four. Sometimes I would come top, sometimes it would be Jayani or Jermaine. Usually we were all pretty much in the same sort of area, just a few thousand votes separating us.

I knew exactly why I wasn't getting the votes I'd had when I did 'Love Life Message'. Partly it was the songs I was being made to do: every week they had a theme and we had to do something within it; stuff like songs from musicals, which I personally think should be banned from human life as evil; Beatles covers, which I always thought shouldn't be allowed as nobody could improve on perfection; and Latin songs, which I kind of liked doing (probably the Spanish in me), but couldn't really get the hang of properly, to do it full justice.

The other issue was the styling. That second week I'd been given a bit of freedom to do my own thing: I got the hair colour I wanted, the cut, plus my clothes were really similar to the ones I would wear on stage with BlackStar, pretty punky stuff, from the cool little shops in the Corn Exchange in Leeds, or down the arcades. Now I was dressed up like some kind of Christmas turkey at times, or in some costume that went with the theme. I hated it.

Still, I knew I had to do as I was told with it all, if I was going to stay in the game: 'In it to win it', as they say, so that's what I did.

We got a few days off over the weekend in the middle of November when the channel switched to its annual charity Saturday night, raising money for kids around the country. It meant that I had a couple of days to relax, even though I still worked hard on the vocals for my next performance, knowing the competition was getting tighter all the time.

Jayani and I decided to do some sightseeing and shopping in London, under heavy disguises, and I invited Kate down to stay over so we could catch up on everything. Jayani looked fab in her razor-sharp straight black wig, totally contrasting with her usual lovely wavy or curly hair. I decided to go blonde for the day, opting for extensions that hid all my darker bits completely. With a bit of 'unusual' make-up and some hilarious clothes that I'd got Kate to bring down from the charity shops in Leeds, we were sorted.

We headed down to Carnaby Street for a bit first, checking out places like Bleach and Marshmallow Mountain, Diesel and Muji, before scooting over to Camden Lock for a rummage around the market. It was great just being out again with nobody recognising me, although I did get a few funny looks. It might have been because I looked like a homeless porn star in my tweedy skirt and hair extensions, who knows? Whatever, it was cool.

'Kate, see this?' I called her over to a stall with Hopi candles and all sorts of other weird spiritual stuff. 'Maybe Britain can get its ears cleaned out instead of voting for the Bolton Brothers every Saturday night.'

We laughed.

'Well, Britain votes for you too, remember, Ell,' Kate whispered into my shoulder.

I punched her lightly on the arm and grabbed her hand before moving over to where Jayani was buying a skin-tight black Lycra top with fake jewels down the front.

'God, that's well nice.' I admired her taste. 'Pity you saw it first or I'd have got it.' I remembered the first rule of shopping with your mates: never ever buy the same outfits . . . she who grabs it, snags it. 'Don't suppose I can borrow it for next week's show, can I?'

Jayani smiled and raised a perfectly plucked eyebrow in my direction.

'In your dreams, honey, in your dreams.' She gave me her best Diva. 'I'm gonna wear it for my performance if they let me, it's gonna wake up all them Asian lads that keep texting in for me. I need to keep 'em on their toes, keep their fingers movin', if you get me.'

I cracked up at her accent and how she deliberately dropped back and forward between American ghetto and Asian Londoner. We were having a great day. It was brilliant seeing Kate again and for her to come and spend some time with Jayani and me. The two of us had become close over recent weeks, and I'd started to enjoy her competitive edge instead of being scared of it. It made for a good combination for the day out, even though *Pop World* seemed to crop up quite a bit in our conversations, at least mine and Jayani's.

'How about we get some lunch? I could murder a burger or something,' Kate suggested.

'I don't mind where we go, as long as it's veggie too,' Jayani replied.

We scanned the high street as we came out of the market area.

'What about "The Good Mixer"?' I suggested, pointing at a pub across the road. 'It's where Blur used to go when they were big. I could sniff one of the chairs and dream.' Damon Albarn was a bit of a hero of mine. I loved the way he's used guitars and rhythm to create a new type of music, especially in Gorillaz.

'Eww, Ellie? And Blur?' Jayani said. 'Who the hell are Blur?'

I rolled my eyes at her, but Kate grabbed my arm just as I was about to answer.

'Forget Blur,' she said. 'Look at that gorgeous guy going into the café over there.'

I took a furtive look. Kate was usually pretty horny about most guys, so I wasn't about to get excited. She usually went for anything in trousers, usually really embarrassing cord trousers, and I wasn't likely to be disappointed this time either. I put her lack of taste down to too many years surrounded by private school boys who liked rugby a bit too much and girls who preferred ponies to human beings, especially male ones.

'Eww, he's well minging, Kate,' I laughed. 'What do you see in these people?'

He was tall and skinny with a pale face and what looked like ginger hair. He was like a puny version of Prince Harry. Too many freckles and the wrong kind of jeans too.

'Well, can we go in there anyway? At least I can stare for a bit while you two get on with talking about your future star life, what you're going to do to win *Pop World*, the usual stuff.' She grinned.

Jayani and I gave her a simultaneous look of horror.

'As if we do. We haven't even mentioned it for . . .' Jayani stopped. 'Erm, oh OK, yeah a minute ago, but . . .' She stopped again, like she'd run out of petrol.

'Am I right?' Kate laughed.

We both nodded sheepishly.

'OK, so let me look at my man, then! And for God's sake, let's talk about something else for a bit when we get there.'

We all linked arms, giggling, and headed across the street into the Jazz Café, ready for some good food and a proper chat.

27

It was hot inside and our faces all went a bit pink after we'd come in from a particularly nippy November London day outside. But it was good to feel all cosy, and in no time at all we were getting all deep and meaningful about life. It helped that we'd had two bottles of red wine between us by then too.

Well, Jayani and I were. Kate was staring at the Harry lookalike.

'Kate, for God's sake, put your tongue back in. He'll think you're a lizard.'

'That's all right for you to say, Ell, you can have any guy you want. You just have to look at them and they fall all over themselves for you.'

Kate seemed to be serious.

'Kate, you're lovely, you just choose the wrong types. You just need somebody, well, good-looking, for instance.' I stifled a giggle.

'Oh please. As if. They never look at me anyway. Look at you and Dylan and Andy. They're both completely in love with you. I never even got a look in with Andy. I've fancied him forever.' Kate was rubbing her hand around the top of her wine glass, absent-mindedly jiggling the remains of her drink from side to side.

'What?' This was news to me. Kate fancied Andy? 'Since when, Kate? You never even mentioned it to me before. I had no idea.'

Kate looked up. 'Well maybe I would have done after you split, but you do get wrapped up in your own problems and your own little world sometimes, Ell. Sometimes you don't consider other people might have stuff going on too.'

I looked into Kate's open, round face, her half-smile not managing to hide the hurt. I knew it must be true if she said it. She was too good a person to say anything she didn't really believe. And she'd given the phone to Andy to talk after persuading him to speak to me that day. How good a friend could somebody be?

'I had no idea, Kate. I'm so sorry. But maybe things can happen for you with Andy now though, I mean, now that we've split up.'

God that sounded arrogant. I hoped she didn't take it like it sounded.

Kate looked down at the glass again and traced her finger round the rim. Jayani made to stand up and murmured about getting another drink, obviously uncomfortable.

'No, it's OK, stay, Jay. I'm fine, I just get down about it sometimes.' Kate paused. I could see she wanted to talk about something else too. It wasn't like Kate to be too serious, although she'd always had her emotional moments.

But this seemed different. There were no tears, just an expression that worried me.

'Is there something else, Kate?' I said, gently, taking her hand in mine.

She sighed and shifted in her seat. 'Yeah, there is. There's a lot more going on than that back home, Ell. It's about Dyl and BlackStar.'

Oh God, what's he done now, I thought. I gave Kate's hand a squeeze. And what about BlackStar?

'Tell me. What's happened?'

Kate took a deep breath and glanced between Jayani and me.

'Good or bad first?' she offered.

'Give me the bad. At least I'll have the good to look forward to.'

'Right, well Dyl's had a pretty bad few weeks. There was a nightmare bit just after you did "Love Life Message" on *Pop World*. He was already getting pissed every night and taking pills, all kind of stuff, and then the press started chasing after him.'

I nodded, my face showing my concern, urging her to continue.

'They were going to his mum and dad's house, to Spirit, all over the place in Leeds, getting people to talk to them about you and him. Mostly him. There were a lot of people that don't like Dyl who took the chance to get a bit of money by saying stuff about his drinking and that. You probably read some of it in the papers.'

I nodded again. 'Yeah, I saw something in the *News* about him, but that's about it. There was a picture of Dyl pissed in a shop doorway. But the producers have kept most of the papers out of the way in the last few weeks and we haven't been able to get out much even if we had a second to ourselves. That's all I really saw.'

'Well, that bit in the *News* was probably one of the best ones. The rest have been really nasty. That was pretty low-key compared to the others. Some people on the music scene in the clubs have been well jealous about you, but especially about BlackStar. They've given the papers stuff about him taking all sorts, which he hasn't done. As far as I know, he's only done pills so far.'

I looked at her in horror.

'Only? God, Kate, that's bad enough. I mean, mixing it with drink as well. He's gonna end up dead if he's not careful. Can't anybody help?'

Kate shook her head quickly.

'Well, he shut virtually everybody out for a while, apart from me and Jamie and Andy, after the worst night when BlackStar played at Spirit.'

I remembered Kate texting me and saying it had been bad, but I hadn't had a chance to catch up with her since.

'It was going really well. They were about three songs in and Dyl was talking to the crowd. He wasn't out of it for once. It looked like it was gonna be a good gig.' She paused and leaned back. 'But you know what Dylan's like. There was a bit of a heckle about his singing being crap from somewhere, so he took the piss back. Next thing you know, the whole crowd were winding him up by chanting.'

I couldn't understand what she was saying. Why would they be chanting?

'In the middle of a gig? What about?' I asked.

'About you, Ell. They were chanting for you and for "Love Life Message". Dylan's said at every gig since you did it that he'd never play it again, and they just wouldn't shut up. So he just totally lost it. He started smashing up his guitar and the amps. We found out later that he'd been on pills and drinking and he was more out of it than we'd thought. In the end Andy had to drag him off stage and get him into the dressing room, and Dylan kept trying to smack Andy until he and Jamie managed to pin him down till he gave up. And there was nearly a riot in the crowd. A lot of their equipment got wrecked, Jamie's too, and people wanted their money back and everything.'

My mouth hung open. I couldn't believe it. As if everything he'd said in the papers hadn't been enough. Now he was behaving like this?

I sat back in my chair.

'Shit,' I said out loud, to nobody in particular. 'He's such a nob, isn't he?' I glanced at Jayani and back at Kate. Kate gave me a bit of a puzzled look, but didn't say any more.

'And what's the good news?'

28

Kate got Jamie to send me BlackStar's press release later that day. It was brief and to the point, but it seemed to be great news for the band. I couldn't help feeling a bit miffed about it all, but at least it might help to get Dylan to pull himself together at last. And Andy deserved whatever good stuff that came his way.

I noticed it didn't mention me. I guessed there must be some sort of contractual reason for that: probably in case *Pop World* sued their asses off.

From: jmeex@hotmail.com
To: lilacswirlzagain@aol.com

Hi Ell,

I've attached what Kate told you about. Good news I reckon:

<u>Kenton James PR</u>

BLACKSTAR UNDER NEW MANAGEMENT

*Following a number of highly successful
tour dates supporting Urban Danser and
the growing public awareness of Dylan
Patrick's songwriting talents through
media outlets such as television, the
Internet and radio, we are pleased to
announce that Kenton James will represent
BlackStar's interests from today.*

*We have been aware of the growing
interest in BlackStar and Dylan Patrick
in the last few months, and feel that we
can steer the band towards success
without compromising their integrity.*

*Incidents publicised in the press in
recent weeks only add to our sense that
BlackStar are a true phenomenon on the
music scene, the genuine article, a band
that is not afraid to work hard, play
hard, and keep that edge that so
powerfully engages with large groups of
young people in Britain today. Dylan
Patrick could accurately be described as
the 'voice of a generation', just like
his illustrious namesake. He is a future
icon, and faces, like all icons do, a
period of time where only those in the*

know, know! We know what Patrick can do, and in time, so will the rest of the world.

Tony MacDonald, our principal manager, who has successfully steered the careers of many top British artists, will represent BlackStar's interests in negotiations for publishing, record contracts, touring and merchandising.

Please note this short biography of band members for use in publications.

© Kenton James Management:

Name: Dylan Patrick
Age: 18
Birthplace: Leeds
Founder of the band, guitarist and song writer
Influences: Chili Peppers, Motown, Massive Attack, Kaiser Chiefs, Andi Peters
Favourite cartoon: The Simpsons
Favourite TV series: Anything with music, nothing from America
Favourite book: Catcher in the Rye by J D Salinger
Favourite film: Apocalypse Now or The Girl Next Door
Favourite band: BlackStar

*Favourite food: Caesar salad . . . yeah
right! Fish and chips*
*Would like to be remembered as: The
band that made music to scribble love
notes to . . .*
*Where do you want to be in 10 years'
time? I want to be playing all over the
world in BlackStar, writing and recording
new material, reinventing ourselves every
time things become normal; I want to be
respected as a musician, married to a
supermodel who loves music and knows how
to make great Yorkshire pudding and
living on a houseboat in Shipley, near
Leeds. Or in a loft apartment in SoHo,
New York. One of the two. I don't mind
which. As long as Leeds are in the
Premier League.*

Name: Andy Moffat
Age: 18
Birthplace: Leeds
Founder of the band, bassist, contributor
*Influences: The Beatles, Arctic Monkeys,
Gorillaz, Kylie, Kaisers.*
Favourite cartoon: Shrek 2
*Favourite TV series: Hit on my
Girlfriend, Big Brother, Match of the Day*
Favourite book: All the Harry Potter

ones; erm they're the only ones I've read
Favourite film: American Beauty or
American Pie, can't remember which
is which
Favourite band: The Deltones (1960s
American soul)
Favourite food: Kebabs from Alt 2 on
Granby Street
Would like to be remembered as: The
world's greatest former-shop-fitter lover
Where do you want to be in 10 years'
time? I want to be in the band still,
playing gigs anywhere they'll have us. I
want to be happy and probably living with
my family (my wife and two or three
kids) somewhere warm maybe, in a nice
house with a big fat car that goes fast.
Oh and can I have shares in Leeds United
too if I've made loads of money, so they
don't get relegated ever again?

Name: Kari Webster
Age: 22
Birthplace: Southampton
Singer, contributor
Influences: Destiny's Child, Sugababes,
anything Garage, R'n'B
Favourite cartoon: Anything Disney
Favourite TV series: 10 Years Younger;

America's Next Top Model; Most Extreme
Makeover
Favourite book: Don't read books. 'Heat'
magazine is where it's at!
Favourite film: Dream Girls
Favourite band: Destiny's Child
Favourite food: Anything that isn't
fattening!
Would like to be remembered as: the new
Kari Webster
Where do you want to be in 10 years'
time? At number one all over the world,
living in a luxury apartment overlooking
the Eiffel Tower in Paris, with Beyoncé,
Madonna and Mariah Carey trying to get me
to do duets to revive their careers.

Please contact Tony MacDonald at Kenton
James for further information.

So what do you think, Ell?
I was a bit surprised they went with Kenton James.
They're not exactly what I'd expected for BlackStar
(bit music BIZ if you get me), but Andy said Dylan
just wanted to get a deal and go with it, and they
signed it after a gig a couple of weeks ago. Seems
they were the first ones that came along with a deal
at the time and when they shoved the paperwork
under their noses, they couldn't wait to sign.

I think Dylan gave up fighting the business when you left. It shook him up, but he's just glad to have a deal now, whoever it's with and whatever it says. Not that I think it's gonna be bad for them. Anyway, they can use this to get a better deal later if they want.

The girl singer seems to have come from nowhere. She's all right, but obviously not a match for you! I think she was signed up to the management company so they drafted her in to replace you quickly.

She even looks like you and they're dressing her up in Ellie clothes. Gotta love show biz eh?!

Anyway, I think all this could pull Dyl round. He's not drinking so much now and he seems a bit more focused. Let's hope so.

Good luck for next week,

J xx

29

By the beginning of December, *Pop World*, and pretty much everything else besides, was beginning to drive me mad.

They'd planned for the final week of the show to happen just before Christmas, partly, I suspected, because young kids were on holiday then and there'd be more time for them to think about texting for their favourites. Also, according to Jayani who'd studied Media at college and seemed to know about stuff like this, it was so that they could get *Pop World* out of the way just in time for the next reality TV show, *Don't Touch Me With That, I'm Famous*. It was the same people they were aiming to get voting in each show, so it didn't pay the TV companies to be competing with each other.

None of this bothered me though. I wasn't fed up because of all the attention and not being able to go anywhere alone any more, even though that was a bit annoying, or the fact that I now had to fight really hard just to stay on the show every week. It wasn't anything positive like the fame. The problem was more that I'd had enough of singing crap songs and wearing crap clothes and being judged on singing things I didn't even like anyway. It was getting me down, and I didn't know if I wanted to carry on. Success was one thing, but this was more like a treadmill every day. The producers had seemed to drop me like a stone after I'd won with 'Love Life Message' and now I was just getting by and scraping through.

It got to the point that I felt like I was going through the motions. I called Mum when I had a spare second between vocal coaching sessions, muting the TV I never watched but left on in the corner as a sort of electric friend.

I'd been told to rest my voice and avoid making unnecessary calls, because I'd developed a bit of a cold the previous week. Screw them, I thought, it's Sunday morning, I'm fed up and I need my mum.

'Hello, Elliana.' I heard the little cough as Mum cleared her throat after saying my name. She always did it. I loved it. It made me miss her so much.

'Hi, Mum, how are you?' I felt like an excited kid. I hadn't talked to her properly in so long, just checking in every now and then for a couple of minutes when I was feeling guilty.

'Oh I'm fine, darling, don't worry about me. Do you think I could call you back in a moment? I'm just sorting out some washing.'

I smiled to myself. I don't talk to her for ages and then she's busy with something little like that when I call. I clicked off the phone and waited till she phoned back.

She sounded great.

'I'm watching you every Saturday and the people from

the papers keep coming to talk to me about you. I think you're doing really well. Everybody tells me you're going to win. I'm voting every Saturday too, don't worry.'

She sounded really cheerful. I wondered what she was trying to hide.

'Really? Aww thanks. Are the papers printing good stuff though, Mum. I don't want them twisting your words. You know what they're like.' I sounded like the mother, not the child.

'No, it's fine. It's just the local ones. They keep writing about you every night, so they send a nice young man over with a notebook and I tell him something nice about you every time. Whatever I tell them it's in there in the next edition.' She chuckled.

My mum wasn't stupid. If she was feeling better, she could do anything she wanted. I hoped this was a sign that things had changed. I had to be careful how I introduced the subject though.

'Are you still getting help from the home help, Mum?' One of the reasons I'd been able to leave was knowing that my mum was getting help from a lady who came to clean and cook for her every day.

'Yes, Cynthia. She's a lovely girl. Always telling me about her children and what they're doing. I tell her a bit about mine too.'

I laughed.

'Cool. And what's going on with the legal papers. Have you sorted all that out?'

I waited. If Mum had finally signed all my dad's stuff, he'd be out of her life at least. Maybe that was why she was sounding better?

'No, darling. I spoke to your uncle in Spain and he's told me not to be bullied. So I'm not signing anything until they come over at Christmas and look at it all for me. But your father is coming here a lot. It's not been very nice.'

My mum was a master of understatement. If my dad wasn't being very nice, that must mean he'd been hassling her and giving her hell. I couldn't understand why she seemed so calm.

'What's he been doing? I'll talk to him. I'll try and keep him away.'

I don't know who I thought I was fooling. I'd never been able to stop my dad doing anything, ever. Luckily she didn't take me up on the offer. She knew him better than I did anyway.

'No, love, don't worry about it. I'm OK just letting him get on with it. He can bang on the windows and doors and make a scene, but I don't let him in. I'm just going to keep on ignoring him and eventually he might stop.'

I thought about my persistent and incredibly controlling father. There was no way he was going to stop any of this.

'Are you scared, Mum?' I asked. I knew my dad had grabbed her before and left marks on her skin. I didn't think he would ever be violent, but I couldn't be sure. He'd scared me before, just with his words.

'No, no, dear. I'm fine. I don't want you worrying. I know you need to concentrate on what you're doing down there. I don't want you distracted by this, so let's talk about you. What's happening there?'

For a split second I was still confused, then I realised what was happening here. My mum had dragged herself together in the couple of minutes before she called me back. And she'd been holding everything together to protect me, to make me think it was OK. It must have taken a lot for her to do that for me.

I wondered if I should say something, but decided if this was the way she wanted it, I needed to respect her. At least she had my Spanish family to help her with Dad now and she did sound at least a bit better than before.

'It's OK, Mum,' I lied. 'I'm getting a lot of help with my vocals from some really good people, and I've learned how to put stage make-up on properly and all that.' I paused, wondering whether to tell her about the terrible rehearsals where I'd stomped out in tears because I didn't want to pretend to be Tina Turner; or the way Martin Harman brushed past me too closely when we met in the corridors, putting a slimy hand in the bottom of my back and moving it around when he was giving me his 'advice'. And what about the fact that even bitchy people on the show's production team had started talking about a new band from Leeds, just loud enough so that I could hear, about how they were still unsigned but getting a real buzz going. They were called BlackStar, and they'd heard they were the new Arctic

Monkeys, even though they'd never even heard a track of theirs.

It seemed like this was all part of being on *Pop World*: bitchiness, back-stabbing, cruelty and stupidity. I wondered how I'd ever thought this could be a good idea and whether I'd done the right thing to do *Pop World* in the first place. I couldn't offload all that on to my mum though, not when she was being so strong for me.

'Oh, that sounds like it's going to be useful, love,' she answered. 'And what about the singing? What are you going to sing on Saturday? I hope it's something I know.'

I laughed. 'It probably will be, Mum; it usually is, isn't it?' I grimaced to myself about the awful songs I'd been singing. 'I don't know, but you know I'm not allowed to tell you anyway, especially now you've got all those friends in the media coming over every day for tea.'

Mum chuckled. 'All I know is that David, the nice lad from the *Mercury*, he said that you're the bookies' favourite to win and be Christmas number one. And you know what they say round here: there are no poor bookies. David says it's yours to lose.'

I groaned inside. Now that was a way to give me some extra confidence. It could have been my dad talking.

'You bet I'm the favourite,' I lied again. 'Jayani's good and Jermaine will get all the girls who fancy him voting, but I'm going to make sure—' Just then I glanced over at the television in the corner of my room, and caught a glimpse of a mop of floppy brown curly hair bouncing up and down in front of the camera, filling the screen. As the camera panned back, it revealed a guitar strung low across a wiry body, and then the face looked straight at me. It was Dylan.

I grabbed the remote from the side table and garbled into the phone.

'Mum, I've gotta go. There's an extra rehearsal I forgot about in a few minutes. They've just called me.'

I felt terrible, but I had to see and hear what was going on. What the hell were BlackStar doing on Channel 4?

I clicked the phone off and perched on the side of my bed, eyes fixed like superglue on the screen, and pressed 'Mute' again, so that the room was filled with the familiar punchy sound of one of our old songs, 'Back of the Market', the one we wrote about this boy called Jason Newlove who I'd snogged one Saturday when I was fourteen round the back of Kirkgate Market in Leeds. My favourite line was 'It's a new love sensation, Didn't give me neck ache oh'. I'd been so proud when we managed to do a daft rhyme of 'sensation' with 'ache oh'. Now I heard the line again, in a voice that could have been mine if I wasn't sitting in a hotel room in London watching it.

'Oh my God,' I whispered out loud. 'They're gonna make it before me.'

The camera panned out again from Dylan and across the small stage to a girl – black-haired, olive-skinned, her pose just like mine used to be – chipping out the words to our song, the song about me. About my love life. My ex-snogfriend.

As the song ended, the incredibly cool guy/girl presenters

147

clapped. I'd never seen them do that before. In all the time I'd watched this programme, every Sunday morning since I was fourteen until just recently, all they'd done was say something funny or sarcastic after the band finished. This time they jumped up and went to talk to the band. To BlackStar. Dylan, Andy and . . . her.

'That was awesome, guys, fantastic,' the male presenter said. I thought he was going to stick his tongue up Dylan's bum the way he was going. 'Mind if we ask you a few questions, or do you have to be "mysterious",' he emphasised the word as if he was being sarcastic, looking at the camera, 'and stay silent till the single and album come out?'

The camera focused across the three of them: Andy, strong, dependable, warm and open as usual, looking exactly like the last time I'd seen him; the new girl singer – Kari, wasn't it? – looking really glam and beautiful, the bitch; and Dylan, totally focused, looking like he did the day I fell for him, the day I first met him. I could have cried.

'We can talk a bit, mate, yeah, we don't get controlled like that, you should know that.' Dylan laughed a little, then looked away, totally cool.

'I know, man, I know,' the presenter gushed.

He turned to the girl.

'Kari, great performance by the way,' he flirted. Kari's face filled up the screen in tight close-up as she beamed at him. 'And is it true that you're all a bit closer than you were when you first got together? Bit of gossip for the viewers maybe?'

148

The screen stayed fixed on Kari's grinning face, before she edged sideways a bit and the camera panned to a wide shot of the three of them. Suddenly I understood what people in accidents say about their life passing before their eyes. Mine did, as Kari's arm slipped out from behind her back and circled around Dylan's shoulder, before she planted a huge kiss firmly on his lips, staring up at him adoringly as he reacted with a full-on love-fest smooch. I felt sick. Then he grabbed her and hugged her, her feet dangling in the air as he picked her up and grinned at the camera and said something to the presenters, who laughed as if it was the funniest joke they'd ever heard. I couldn't hear anything. All I could see was the girl I used to be, holding the man I used to want to be with. She might as well have been holding my ripped-out bloody heart in her hands, the way she'd so totally destroyed me.

'OK, that's so cool, fantastic.' The presenter looked jealous. 'But can you not just get a room?' The presenters laughed again and Dylan rolled his eyes sheepishly. I tried to focus on what they were saying, to mask what I was feeling.

'So, Dylan, back to the band: can you tell us the date it's all going to happen then? There's been a buzz around your first release for weeks, around the whole band really, and now our research down the pub with you lot last night tells us you're bringing out your first recorded material, simultaneously,' he emphasised the word by shouting it out as if it was some kind of great theory of scientific discovery, a eureka moment, 'as a single and an album, a first in pop history from what we can make out.'

Dylan ran his hand along the neck of his guitar, producing a bit of amp screech along the way, and then settled almost disdainful eyes back on the presenter, as if a bit bored by the question. He was a rock star already. But then, he always had been.

'Yeah, they're out the week before Christmas, December 17th I think, both together. We're releasing them together cos we're ready to, no other reason. People might say it's about hype but it isn't. We just want to do it cos they're both well good. You won't be disappointed.'

He smirked. He was like a beautiful Liam Gallagher, all attitude and brooding presence, none of the dumbness. I could see the confidence dripping off him. God they all looked good. It was awful.

'What's the first single gonna be, Dylan?' the presenter asked.

'Not sure yet,' he replied, 'but probably one of our new songs we've been working on. They're better than anything we've done before.' Dylan looked directly at the presenter, for the first time in the interview. He looked like he meant business.

New songs? Did the new girl have anything to do with writing BlackStar songs as well? Had I been taken over by an alien life-form called Kari? It just got worse and worse.

A few seconds later, the programme moved on. New faces filled the screen, new sounds filtered into my consciousness.

But I hadn't moved on at all. I sat and looked out at the

grey, damp London morning, mist and drizzle picking away at my window in tiny flecks of water. It felt like I'd been sitting there for hours, but it was probably just a few minutes at the most. I didn't know what to do. I knew I couldn't cry, the tears weren't there, even though I felt like I needed to. I looked down at the phone still sitting cradled in my hand, and gently placed it back on the side table beside my bed.

This wasn't fair.

It wasn't supposed to be like this.

Wasn't I supposed to be the star?

30

I made my mind up to leave that afternoon.

After I'd gone to see the main producer, I stopped by Jayani's room down the corridor. She was practising scales.

'What?' was all she could say. Over and over.

I tried to explain. She knew all about Dylan, BlackStar, Andy and my mum. It was all too much, and I felt like I needed her to understand, if I was going to be able to do this. If Jayani could understand, somebody who was more like me than anybody I'd ever met, then perhaps I was doing the right thing after all.

'I just think you're making a huge mistake,' she said, eventually, once she'd got past the shock. 'I mean, when are you gonna get another chance like this, babes? We're down to four this weekend and you know we'll both be there, and look at Gareth and Will, they both ended up having careers even though one of them had to win in the end. We're gonna be the female Gareth and Will!'

It wasn't the first time she'd made the comparison with the legendary TV pop contestants. Even though it was all years ago now, we all knew they set the standard for everybody that followed. In fact Jayani had gone around stuttering for a couple of days early on in the competition, while I pretended to sing in a really high poncey voice like Will, only to realise we were upsetting people loads and being a bit cruel. We still did it in private a bit every now and then though and it always made us laugh.

'Just think about it overnight, yeah?' she pleaded. 'I mean, just ask yourself why you're here, what you did this for. We're the same, you and me. And I wouldn't leave here now for anything. So you can't either.'

I thought a lot about what she said. The producers had begged me to do the same. They seemed more upset than I was at the thought that I might go. In the end I decided they were right. I had to sleep on it.

The morning didn't get me any closer to being sure, so I called my dad and arranged to meet him at midday. He was staying in London anyway, on one of his many business trips, and as soon as he heard the basics of my dilemma, he agreed we needed to talk. And if anyone had an opinion on this, it would be him.

Obviously Dad knew that there was plenty of stuff I was capable of doing instead of *Pop World*, even if BlackStar wasn't an option any longer, and it didn't have to be in the music business. He'd always loved the idea of helping to make me 'a starry star', as he used to call it, but used to drum into me that I needed a 'fall-back position', just in case, so that I could be the best in whatever I did. He'd made sure that the law was the favourite if everything else failed. Knowing him like I did, I was sure he'd push for me to stay, but I still wanted to hear what he had to say. For all his faults, he was my dad, and he could think clearly in a crisis, even if it was usually about how he could get himself in the lifeboat first.

He picked me up at the hotel in a taxi and we drove into central London.

'I've got a treat for you. I've hired somewhere that we can talk privately for a while, so that you can clear your head and come to some good conclusions. I've ordered some lunch for us, and a few drinks. By the time we finish, you'll be sorted. So stop worrying.' He smiled warmly. 'Here we are.'

We stopped in a side street near the Thames and stepped out into a wide concourse that seemed to appear from nowhere. Directly above me, huge and imposing, was the London Eye. I stared at it for a few seconds, trying to take in the amazing structure, the size of it and how it hung there, like it was a giant bangle clinging to the riverside, before looking back at my dad.

'Dad, what have you . . .?'

He shushed me.

'Come on. We've got a capsule. It's something I do when clients come in from America and the Far East. They love it. Never fails to tie up the deals I'm brokering. Hurry up; we're booked in in five minutes' time.'

I stared at him in wonder. You had to give him credit, he had some class. Maybe he was where I got it from?

Whatever happened, I was going to make this decision in

154

style. I skipped after him as he strode through the damp wind towards the capsule station, wrapping my big coat and scarf around me against the chill. He pulled me towards him, hugging me tightly as we waited for our spaceship capsule to land.

31

The London skyline below us seemed to be softened behind tiny droplets of damp air that gathered on the capsule as we slowly turned. Perhaps this city wasn't the harsh place I'd started to think of it as, after all? I gazed out as far as the mist would let me: the huge arc of Wembley Stadium in the distance to the north, aeroplanes coming in to land at Heathrow in the west. The view was even better than the one from True Radio's studios.

I glanced across at my dad, leaning against the handrail in his expensive suit, the manicured sandwiches laid out behind him in our private capsule. Sometimes it was great having a corporate lawyer for your father: where else would I have been able to go to escape today with the press everywhere around the hotel, even with one of my many disguises on? We'd shaken the press off as soon as the taxi had joined the London commuting traffic and I was so grateful for a bit of peace and some time to think.

And I knew I could get used to luxury like this. A bottle of champagne rested lazily in a bucket of ice on the table. Reclining chairs had been carefully placed so that we could make the most of the views whilst we gobbled up everything that was on offer. The perfection inside our little pod was completed by an overwhelming sense of peace. All I could hear was the gentle swishing of whatever it was that made this thing move; oh and the gentle swishing of the cogs of my brain still trying to make the right decision. That hadn't gone away despite all my dad's best efforts.

I turned away from the view to face him.

'I've got to decide what I'm doing by four. Sandra said the producers will call a press conference if I'm going. Even she was saying I should sort myself out. God, she's such a witch.'

I pouted. It usually got me some sympathy from Dad, at least for a while. Today he seemed a bit indifferent. His mood seemed to have got darker since we'd got in to the capsule.

'OK, let's just sit down and talk it through,' he said in a quiet, businesslike tone. 'We've got three rotations if we need them, that's ninety minutes. Plenty of time to make a good decision.'

Ninety minutes? I thought to myself. This could take a lifetime. Or I could regret it for a lifetime. One of the two.

Dad nodded encouragingly. I was surprised at how well he was taking this. Normally he would have gone off on one by now and ended up telling me to get on with it and stop moaning. It was all a bit suspish really, but I was hoping his sensitive side was kicking in for once.

'Right. Off you go. Tell me all about it,' he said.

I looked into his broad, pale face, his cheeks a bit

reddened by the cold. I loved him so much, despite everything he'd done to Mum and me and the way he sometimes was. Why did he have to be like that, when he could be like this? This was so much better.

'There's so many things going on, Dad, I don't even know where to start.' I could feel a pricking in my eyes. The peace and the space and the warmth in my dad's decision to get me here was having an effect, as well as finally having to think about everything that had started to overwhelm me these last few days and weeks. I hadn't cried for years, but it felt like everything was on the brink of gushing out, all the feelings I'd been storing up. I felt myself begin to blush at the thought of crying in front of my dad. And then I felt myself begin to blush at the thought of it being bad to blush in front of your own dad. What kind of family was I part of?

'Take your time,' he offered, reaching into his pocket. 'Here's a hankie.'

I could see a hint of distaste in his face that I was becoming emotional.

Eww, a hankie?

I took a deep breath and tried to even out my breathing, performing the exercises the vocal coach had taught me to control my nerves.

'OK.' I composed myself. Letting it all out to my dad was not something I was used to. It wasn't something I was used to doing with anyone, not even Kate, but it had to happen. I couldn't make this decision on my own. It was too huge.

'I'm starting to think this was a huge mistake, Dad. I

thought it would get me what I've always wanted, all the fame and the attention, and that I'd love being around people like me who want it more than anything, but actually, it's not like I thought it would be.' I glanced up at him, praying I hadn't already lost his attention. It wouldn't have been the first time he'd drifted into his own thoughts the minute I started to say something important to me. He was way easily distracted at times, especially when he wasn't the main subject of the conversation. But he seemed to be focused now.

'The people are so fake, even the producers. I don't believe a word they tell me now. After that second week when everything went mad, they were all over me, and now I just feel like they don't give me enough support and they make me sing stupid songs I hate, and then Jayani gets better coaching and advice from the judges and special meetings with the producers and then she ends up with everyone loving her. I just don't understand it any more.'

I paused to take a breath. Dad looked surprised. He'd never seen me quite this wound up and babbling. Well only once: the day he'd left us. And even then it hadn't taken me long to get my shit together and realise I was the one looking after things now.

'Go on . . .' he said.

I looked out of the capsule and it all came flooding out. For some reason, I couldn't stop it, and it felt right to let go.

'And that's the biggest thing out of all of this. I'm just singing crap songs that I hate, and I don't even know who I am any more. One week I'm supposed to be an "all-round entertainer", that's what they call it, the next I'm supposed to be a "bar-room chanteuse". I don't even know what a "chanteuse" is, Dad. I just went along with what they told me to do. I mean as if I'd ever wear a feather boa, for God's sake. I'm from Leeds.'

He laughed and then stifled it behind his hand.

I looked up at him.

'It's not funny, Dad, this is serious.' Typical. The one time I finally pour my heart out, he thinks it's a joke. It's not surprising I'd hidden everything from him forever.

'I know it's not, love. If only your audience could see you now,' he smiled. He liked taking the mick. He always seemed at his most comfortable when making fun of people, even if it was gently.

I got out a tissue and dabbed the sides of my eyes. They were still dry, but I was worried about my make-up running. I decided I needed to say all this, no matter how bad his listening skills were.

'You can't even imagine what it's like being in that hotel as well, week after week, nobody to talk to cos you don't get home till after midnight some nights, and you're knackered, so you just flop down on the bed and fall asleep ready for the next morning when you start singing at eight. It never stops. And then the next day you get up and people who don't even know you tell you you're crap at things you thought you were good at, and you start to think you are crap, when a few weeks ago I thought I was brilliant. I can't stand it.'

I took a deep breath in and continued, my voice wobbling a bit as I tried to control my emotions.

'There's other stuff as well. Stuff with Andy and Dylan and that girl that they've got to be me. They're doing really well, Dad. What if I've made a huge mistake? What if I lose and I've got nothing and they get even bigger and I look like such an idiot for quitting them and thinking I was so special that I could make it big on my own?'

I could feel the tears beginning to form in my eyes. I leaned forward with my head over my knees so that they would fall straight on the floor instead of running down my cheeks.

I felt Dad's arms around my shoulders. I thought about shrugging them off. I'd never had him comfort me, never needed him to, but this time I just let them stay there, strangely comforted by their heaviness. I started to sob, quietly, almost afraid of what he would say.

'You've just got yourself into a negative state of mind, Ellie. It wouldn't be the first time, would it?' Dad sighed, impatience creeping into his voice now. He sounded awkward, like the tiniest bit of sympathy in his words was forced. Not that I could hear much sympathy anyway. It just sounded like more criticism of me, as usual. 'You'll see, all this . . .' he paused, looking for the right word, '. . . nonsense will pass and then you'll get all your old determination and fight back. Finally.'

I sensed another subtle change of tone, a bit of sarcasm, maybe? Perhaps it was too much to ask that the tiny bit of kindness he'd shown could continue? It wasn't like he had much experience of giving it, and if it had truly been there, it was well out of character. His voice hardened as he removed his arms and stood up, walking over to the window. He looked like Real Dad again. Fake Nice Dad must have left the building. Against all my instincts, I couldn't stop the tears. I fought it, but they only came faster now.

I didn't want to look at him, knowing too well from experience the darkness that would now have descended over his eyes. I waited, not answering. There was probably going to be an explosion after all. How could I have thought there wouldn't be, after all the evidence of my whole life?

Dad paced across the capsule towards me and stood right in front of my down-turned face.

'Ellie, look at me for God's sake, and stop bloody crying.' He reached towards my hands as they covered my face, trying to pull them away so that I would look at him. I kept them firmly in place. 'What the hell is wrong with you? Where's the Batchelor in you gone? You're behaving like your bloody mother. Stop snivelling.'

His tone was angry now, impatient.

'I've never thought of you as a quitter, Ellie. Quitting's for little babies, remember? Haven't you listened to anything I've been telling you for all these years?'

It was one of Dad's old sayings. He'd come up with it one weekend when I was eight. I'd been rehearsing a dance routine all weekend in the basement for a big competition, but I wanted to watch *The Simpsons* before I went to bed on the Sunday evening and my ankle was hurting from a fall I'd had the week before in my gymnastics class. He'd made me do another hour of practice because of that, and kept the extra hour for every practice from then on, to teach me that I needed to 'commit', if I was going to make anything of myself. I'd needed a pain-killing injection the following weekend before I could compete. I still won.

If I'd had any idea what commitment actually meant then, I might have mentioned the irony of somebody like him using the word. But I was only eight. It was all coming back to me now, though: his betrayal of my mum, his bullying of both of us over the years. How could I have thought this would actually help?

'And quit rhymes with something else too. Don't let me down like this, Ellie, you're not a baby.'

I looked up to find his face contorted in a suppressed rage. He'd always been worried about what people would think, desperate to avoid anyone thinking there was a chink in his armour I guess, so Batchelor arguments were organised carefully so that they happened in private. Our old stone detached house in Leeds was perfect for that. You could shout as loud as you wanted and nobody would hear. But here we were completely alone, except for the people in the next capsule, and they could see us, but they definitely couldn't hear. For some reason, his cold, menacing look and quiet anger made him even scarier now than when he shouted and screamed at my mum in the old days.

From somewhere, I found a voice and the words came

tumbling out, things I'd wanted to say for ever, but never had the guts to.

'It's always about you, isn't it? What you've done, what you've said. And don't talk about Mum like that. She's better than you'll ever be. Just because you're a big-shot lawyer and you think you can boss everybody around, it doesn't make you a better person. You're horrible to me and to Mum and anybody who gets in your way. At least Mum cares about me and not just about what I can do to make her look good. All you care about is yourself and your own stupid life. You're a . . . bas—'

I wanted to say it, but I couldn't quite get it out. It was a word that had been on my lips for years, ever since he'd left, but I still couldn't say it to him. It just wouldn't come out of my mouth. He was standing right above me now, and I felt his hot breath as he leaned in towards me. I sensed his shock at what I'd said. And maybe what I hadn't.

'Oh you think so, Elliana? And I suppose that your mother has helped you come to this wonderful conclusion about your own father? After everything I've done for you, all the years of ferrying you around and helping you with your work and your practices, when your mother was sat at home being "depressed" or whatever she came up with that week.' He paused. I felt as though it was raining heat and pain.

'You're an ungrateful, spoiled brat. You sit there telling me I'm selfish, when it's you that gave up a job that anybody would die to have, that I'd laid on a plate for you.' He was

164

on a roll now. I'd seen it enough to know this wasn't going to end quickly. 'And I supported you to follow your dreams, gave you ballet lessons, singing lessons, tutoring for your schoolwork, computers, a bloody personal recording studio in your bedroom, in the house that I paid for and I'm not allowed to live in any more. And you call me selfish?'

I fixed my eyes on the rubber flooring beyond the edge of the capsule carpet. I wasn't interested in the view any more. It was ugly. Everything in this place was ugly.

'And now look at you. All you can do is snivel and cry and give up, just because it involves a little bit of a challenge. A little bit of inconvenience in your privileged life that I've worked all the hours God sent to pay for. Listen to me.' He waited for me to look up, but I kept my eyes fixed to the floor. 'Listen to me,' he shouted, close to my face, making me jump. I felt my body begin to tremble in fear.

I looked up at him, trying to focus and show some sort of defiance in the face of his attack.

'You're no daughter of mine if you give up on this now. You get on with it, do it right and sort yourself out. Get over yourself, Ellie, you don't have a right to give up, I've invested too much in you already, and I want some return on it now, I want something back for once.'

He pulled himself up straight again. I stared as his face lost its anger, but not its colour, almost purple with the rage he'd failed to control. From under my eyelids I could see him straightening his tie under his jacket and smoothing down the lapels.

'And don't you ever dare to speak to me like that again. Ever. Do you understand me?'

I wiped my eyes with the back of my hand and stared into his, mine now empty of emotion, controlled again, blotting out the pain. I felt rooted to the chair, as if pinned by an invisible set of stakes.

And I thought of my mum, back in Leeds, and of her chair, her eyes, her emptiness. And my mind went blank.

32

All I could hear was the electric humming of the circular light fitting above my head, as it bathed the room in its murky-yellow, puke-coloured blanket. Sealed off from the outside world by plastic skirting boards, thick tiled walls and the heavy wooden door that led into the bedroom, I slumped against the side of the bath on the floor of my hotel bathroom, the tears from the capsule ride long since dried up.

The floor was warm against my bum, which had felt weird for the first hour or so, because for all these weeks I'd thought the floor was made out of tiles and weren't tiles supposed to feel cold? But the whole room was warm, hot even. I tried to force a fingernail into the sides of one of the tiles, to pick it apart, but realised they were all moulded together, plastic like a piece of lino or something. I'd walked on this floor countless times and never even registered that it wasn't real. It had seemed so luxurious to have my own bathroom in a hotel, tiled and warmed like a cosy little escape from the busy world outside. But I guess the tiles were fakes, just like everything and everybody else in this world.

I didn't know how long I'd been there, huddled up in just my bra and pants, thinking, and then trying not to think. The minutes had turned into hours without me really registering them. My body and my mind were numb, for the first time in my life, like there was nothing going on in my mind, no questions, no plans, no ideas. The spinning, conflicting, rushing thoughts of a few hours ago had seemed to push and haul and drag me this way and that, until even they had given up, maybe realising that I had no more energy to fight them or anything else any more. They'd exhausted themselves inside me, inside exhausted me. There was nowhere to go with this. I'd given up.

The steam in the room from the bath had long since dispersed and the water must be lukewarm now, no longer giving off its wisps of boiling vapour, but I felt clammy, my body still damp from the hot, moist air of the room, my hands sweating from the heat pounding out of the radiator at my feet. I stretched out again, vaguely aware of the aching in my bum from the hard floor, shifting position for the hundredth time, but not wanting to get up. Getting up meant facing this, facing the world.

I stared down at my naked feet and legs, the all-over-tan leaving no lines and no streaks as my eyes followed them towards my thighs. My mind briefly flickered back to the empty cubicle at the salon, where I'd stood five times now, waiting for my 'body technician' and her spraying equipment to start colouring me in, turning me 'Kiss of Indian Summer' all over, nothing left uncovered, nothing left as me. The first time I'd gone, I'd asked why a girl with olive skin needed a tan. The woman had just looked at me as if I was mad, as if it was such a stupid question, I couldn't possibly want an answer to it.

I held my right hand in my lap, the left tucked between my thighs, and tried to focus in on the little downy hairs that covered my wrists, the ones I used to be so self-conscious about when I was younger, before I realised that everybody has them and it wasn't because I was a bear. My eyes traced up along the delicate lengths of my fingers, manicured like some high-flying London businesswoman in her thirties, right to the bright red Mac-covered nails, the polish, or varnish, or lacquer or frost, Virgin Rouge or whatever the make-up artist had called it, gleaming brightly in the yellowy light like blood seeping from an open wound.

I lifted my left hand from its resting place, turning those fingers towards me in wonder, opening their grip again and stretching them, staring with fear, excitement, shock. What? What was I feeling?

I couldn't feel anything, I could only see. There didn't seem to be a reason for any of this: the hotel room, the London Eye, the press outside in the street, the twenty-seven phone messages and texts from the producers before I'd even got back to my room, the stupid songs, the ridiculous fake tan, the girl on the floor in the hot bathroom in her pants that seemed to be somebody else . . .

Except I knew there was a reason why I'd put the shining silver scissors from my make-up bag into my hand; and there was a reason why I'd run the bath; and there was a reason why I'd gone into the bathroom and locked the door.

And I knew that the points of the scissors were starting to make sharp imprints on my wrists for a reason, too.

I put my fingers into the holes in the scissors again, and opened them up, before grasping them firmly in my right hand again, the blades now forming the shape of knives at right angles to each other, one point pressing into my skin creating a tiny volcano which was just about to erupt.

On the floor next to the sink, my mobile buzzed for the millionth time, and I ignored it again, focusing instead on the silver scissors glinting in the glow of the light.

And the clock on the wall said it was half-past three.

33

Daily News:
Jessie Martin's CelebrityGossipZone 4 December 2008

REACHING FOR THE BLACKSTARS

They haven't even had a single out yet, although that's soon to change, and when it does, you'll know everything there is to know about pop's next big thing.

We hear Kari, Dylan and Andy have been working hard on their new single and album for a couple of weeks now, in between regular visits to London's uber-cool venues for the glitterati, photo-shoots with Damien Price at the V and A, and a bit of schmoozing with the big boys at Abbey Road studios and the fashion editors of the glossies around Shoreditch.

The single is still up in the air though. Although everybody around BlackStar world wants the band to release their version of

'Love Life Message', the hugely successful track performed by former lead singer Ellie Batchelor on a recent Pop World, Dylan Patrick refuses to have anything to do with his most famous song.

'It's just another BlackStar track,' he commented, 'something we used to do but don't need to any more because we've evolved. Just wait till you hear the rest of the stuff on the new album.'

Patrick confidently predicts that we'll soon forget all about Ellie Batchelor, once the BlackStar album hits the streets just before Christmas. 'She's history now, and she's not even doing that well on Pop World either. Maybe she realises what a big mistake that was now. But the important thing for us is to get the music out there and start gigging. We do things properly, and we'll make it our way, without a load of music business crap going on in the background, and our fans have known that for a long time.'

Real 'Working Class Hero' stuff from Dylan. So let's hope it all works out for them. Can you imagine if the single stiffs?!

Tom Macdonald, experienced manager of

the *fledgling superstars, suggests that
there's no chance of that happening. He's
guided the careers of a whole series of
top performers across Europe, including
Red Sun, The Brainwaves and Sesame. Now he
feels he's got the biggest of the lot and
Internet interest proves his point.*

*'We're the biggest site on MySpace right
now, more visits than The Vatican's new
PopeNet site and growing every day. If
we're beating a whole religion, we've got
to be doing something right,' he laughed.
'And we can't wait to translate it into
sales. Hopefully Christmas will be big for
us. And there's no way that Ellie Batchelor
can compete with our platform. Martin
Harman will be disappointed with whoever
wins Pop World this year, when he sees
what he's missed with BlackStar. This is
real music. And Kari Webster is a real
star in the making. She's beautiful,
talented, and a winner!'*

*It seems we're in for a busy few weeks
in the pop charts, especially if Batchelor
somehow pulls out an unexpected win on Pop
World. That seems unlikely since she only
just scraped into this Saturday's final,
and she's been keeping a low profile, not*

even speaking to the press. Not the best way to win friends eh? But she'll be keeping her fingers crossed that she can turn it round somehow.

Here at CelebrityGossipZone, we're rooting for Jayani . . . bootie calls us whenever we see her and she's always welcomed us into her fabulous world. We'll keep you posted with all the pop gossip all this week as always . . .

34

I deleted my email account, changed my SIM and shut down my BlackBerry. Apart from the *Pop World* team, only my mum knew how to contact me now, and I made her swear on the Virgin Mary that she wouldn't give my number out to anybody, not even Kate or Jamie. She promised me she wouldn't. I copied my contacts list to my new SIM then deleted all my dad's numbers. I wouldn't be speaking to him again in a hurry.

I'd sat with those scissors in my hand for what seemed like forever, until the room phone had rung and dragged me out of my fog. I didn't want to get it, but it kept on and on, and the only people who had the number were the production team. It was quarter to four. They'd wanted their decision.

In the end it had been easy. I stood up, walked to the phone and answered. Within a few minutes, I was back on the show. It was Martin Harman, personally calling me to talk. I pulled myself together, dragged on a bathrobe and listened to what he had to say.

'Ellie, listen to me. You can't quit now. We have such high

hopes for you. There will come a time when you understand that everything happens for a reason, but right now it just seems like a lot of hard work and it's all getting too much for you. But you're young and it'll get easier.' He paused as his words sunk in. I had hardly breathed while he spoke, terrified that whoever was calling needed to hear my decision, the decision I still hadn't made.

'Ellie, I want you to be in my stable of artists,' he continued. 'You're a star. I've got no doubts about that. I saw it the first day I met you and heard you sing, up in Manchester. And when we met and talked, it was like you were one of my girls already.'

I sat down on the bed, my ear glued to the phone and the sharp, professional voice at the other end. Sure he could be pervy and slimy, but he knew what he was talking about, and right now, the only thing that was clear in my mind was that a sophisticated, experienced and hugely successful music producer was telling me I still had a career, despite everything else in my life being messed up and failing. It felt like it could be enough for me.

'And whatever happens, there will be a place for you with me. I promise you. Who knows what'll happen on Saturday? Even if you don't win, and I think you will, you will have a contract, trust me.' I gripped the phone tighter. 'But only if you continue on the show. I can't offer you anything, win or lose, if you quit. I wouldn't be able to justify it to my fans. I have my reputation to keep.'

I grunted a noise that showed I'd understood,

even though I couldn't speak yet. He seemed to know I needed more.

'If you commit to this, Ellie, I'll make you a star. I'll help you this week and after that with everything. I'll protect you from the media, your ex-friends who I keep reading saying bitchy things about you, your family if you need me to. Anybody you don't want to talk to, I'll keep away. I'm going to organise everything from now on, right down to when you brush your teeth in the morning, and what colour socks you wear. So all you have to do is focus on your singing and your career. What do you think?'

I could hardly speak. It felt like the hours of fear and pain were slipping away, replaced by something clear and straightforward, something I could hold on to, something that was easy to take and believe and hold on to.

'You'd do that for me? Even if I don't win? You'd give me a contract?' I spoke hoarsely, almost whispering.

'Yes I will. And in return I will expect you to do exactly what I say. I'll work everything out so that it's all for your benefit, but I need your agreement. This is between us, remember. Now what's your answer? We've got to call that press conference within five minutes if you're leaving, so that we can catch the dailies tomorrow.'

I knew it was the right thing to do. I thanked him, feeling more grateful for this than for anything I'd ever achieved in my life. It was like a huge sack of crap was being lifted from my shoulders all at once.

'OK, just stay in your room. I have my PA coming over

in two minutes, and I will be there in twenty. I'm at the studios right now. Tonight, I'm going to present you with your plan for the next six months of your life.'

The phone clicked and he was gone. I lay back on my bed and closed my eyes. It was going to be OK after all, better than OK. I just needed to stop worrying, let Martin and his team look after me and be strong and it would all come to me, instead of me fighting it and trying to work it out for myself.

I turned over for a second and hugged the pillow, allowing myself a deep sigh and a tiny smile of relief, as I heard a firm knock on the door.

35

Martin was true to his word over the next couple of days, organising everything right down to the tiniest detail. I started to warm to him, especially as his hands had stopped wandering quite so much, though still a little bit too close to areas that I considered 'out-of-bounds' at times. But I figured that it was the price I was going to have to pay to get myself where I wanted to be. And there were worse people to be groped by. He was actually quite a funny guy, once you got past the image he put up for the public, and he made a lot of sense when he talked about my career and the future.

On the Wednesday of the final week, we had a meeting in my hotel room, the safest place to avoid members of the production staff at *Pop World*, and paparazzi photographers who were all over London like a rash, forever trying to get pictures of him, according to Harman. There was Martin, his PA Melissa, me and Sandra. I'd assumed that Sandra was going to be phased out after our little agreement, because she worked for *Pop World* not Martin, but it didn't seem to bother him to have her there, and she seemed pretty comfortable about it too. In fact, it was the first time

I'd seen her relax since she'd started minding me. I figured that they must have been working pretty closely for *Pop World* since it started all those years ago, and that she was trustworthy.

'OK, first of all the rules. These are the absolute basics. Break these and the deal is off.'

I nodded and waited intently.

'One, I don't want you talking to Jayani any more, other than to be pleasant. She's your number one rival for the show, and even though I'm judging, there are still two more judges, plus a whole public out there to choose her, and the last thing I want is for her to be putting you off and making you less than razor sharp. You will win this if you fight her, but not if you're distracted. Understand?'

I nodded. My friendship with Jayani had always been against my better (or should I say, killer?) instincts, but she'd been too nice to push away before. But if I had to do it, I would. I could see Martin's point.

'Two, *Pop World* is moving you to Central London tonight, and each of you will be in a different hotel from the other contestants. It means they feel they have more control over you, but actually it gives me the chance to see more of you and work with you. So I have taken out a suite there under a different name. Nobody can know where you are staying, except me and the *Pop World* team. I don't even want your parents to know, understand? This is proper Boot Camp now. You need total emersion in the competition if we're to pull it round.'

I smiled. 'I've been desperate to get out of here for days. Bring it on.'

'OK, good. Three, I hear from the production team that contestants have been given a choice of what songs to do in the final, a new one plus something you've already covered in the series. And you're in two minds about what songs you're going to do?'

I nodded again. It was something I'd been worrying about for days.

'There is no question about it. I'll sort out the new one. And you're doing "Love Life Message". It was your best song, it's original, it's brilliant, and it suits your style to perfection. It's you. You will be comfortable singing it, and when you do win, note I said "when", it will be your first single. I've decided. So you'll do it once during the show, and then for your encore when you win, just after they announce the release date, which will be just in time for the Christmas Number One. *Your* Christmas Number One.'

He seemed to have it all worked out, and I loved his confidence in me. God knows I needed it right now. I had other worries about the song though.

'Martin, there's the problem with copyright. I didn't write it, remember? I don't think Dylan would let me do it now. He's bound to have copyrighted it to himself by now.'

Harman looked up for a moment and held my eye. He appeared annoyed.

'Ellie, what did I tell you about leaving everything to me? I've sorted everything out. You should know that I wouldn't leave any loose ends. I sort everything out. Everything. OK?'

I brightened up. It was such a huge relief knowing that I could do the song again. Now I couldn't wait to perform in the final.

'OK, I hear you.' I grinned. 'You're a lot easier to work with than everybody thinks.'

Harman glanced up from the papers that covered my bed and winked.

'It gets easier the more we get to know each other.'

I smiled again, this time with a little more effort.

'Any more rules?' I asked.

'Four. You will stay in your new room at all times when you're not in preparation for the show on Saturday. I've already had the phone line and the TV removed from there, the papers cancelled. I've had a sound system installed, and the room is big enough to allow us to prepare your stage routine for "Love Life Message". I want you in there rehearsing, doing your exercises, practising scales, learning words. This week is all about focus. In the time you're not sleeping, either Sandra or Melissa will be in contact. Sandra is going to be just next door. Apart from them, you won't be talking to anybody this week. Agreed?'

I nodded again. I'd made my own decision about this anyway. I wanted nothing more than to concentrate, with no distractions, no feelings, no worries. It wasn't like Jamie or Kate or anybody back home had tried to protect me from Dylan and the band and the snidey little comments they'd been making all over the place. I felt like I was back in the basement practising for a dance competition, all alone, depending on me again, but this time it was all on my own terms and I didn't have Dad forcing me to do it, and then taking the credit.

'Good. That's it then. Actually, there is one last thing. Remember that this is a private agreement at the moment: if anybody at the studios finds out, I'll just deny it all and you will be made to look a fool. I'm a lot more powerful than anybody there . . .' he paused, frowning, 'and especially anybody in this room.' He tilted a warning eyebrow in my direction. 'And I want you to practise four or five songs at the studios, so that they don't know which ones you're going to do. Make it look as though you probably won't be doing "Love Life Message". Mess it up, make it ragged whenever they get you to rehearse it. We'll do all of the work on that one here, through Melissa and myself, whenever I can get to visit.'

Melissa started to gather the papers from the bed. Obviously she'd known in advance exactly when the meeting would be ending. Her hair was tied back in a formal ponytail, and she was perfectly made up. She looked like a doll.

'Thank you so much, Martin,' I gushed. 'You've been fantastic.'

He smiled as he stood, much taller than he seemed behind the judging desk on screen, always surprising you with his powerful size.

'Don't mention it. We'll do this together, and then anything is possible.'

He reached across and pecked me on the cheeks, one on each side, the second hesitating for just a second too long against my skin, before moving to the door. Sandra checked the corridor before they all stepped out and left me alone again, excited about what was to come.

I thought for a moment about the song I was going to sing, and how Dylan might feel when he found out it was going to be my first single. He'd be gutted, that was for sure.

But I knew he deserved everything he got. He'd been screwing me over in the media for weeks, and had brought in a girl who might as well have been me, without the talent of course. And if he was going to be an idiot and didn't want to sing the song, just because I'd made it 'dirty' by singing it instead, then I would. Again and again. And I'd use it to get back at him and Andy, and Kari Webster, or whatever her name was, for everything.

I pulled the long sleeves of my top back over my wrists and rubbed the insides gently. There were some tiny marks, like pin-pricks, that were red and sore, angry but not broken. There were no fresh scars, no wounds. There had been no need in the end. I'd come out of the darkness.

I'd seen Kari Webster and Dylan Patrick and Andy Moffat in my head, and I'd realised that it was going to have to be them or me. I could give in and disappear, or fight back and win.

It was simple.

The only way I could succeed was if they were destroyed.

36

From: jmeex@hotmail.com
To: katiebum89@bluestreak.com

Where the hell are you when I call you? I've been
trying all day and texting. You're never there these
days and I'm just hoping you've not gone back to
that sad twat Jonathon.

I'm gonna have to fill u in on all the shit that's been
happening down here by email instead. You better
call when u get this. Soooo much to tell u lol. You
won't believe what's been happening.

I got here on Tuesday and hung out with Dyl and
Andy at the rehearsal studios. They've signed them
up for a major tour after Christmas . . . it looks like
they think the single's gonna be massive cos they're
playing all the big venues and some of the summer
festivals. It's all sorted for BlackStar now. I can't
believe how big it's got now they're with that agency.

That's the good news. There's so much shit going down tho, I don't know if the tour and everything is gonna be worth it in the end.

I went to the studio on Wednesday and we were hanging out with Tony Macdonald's PA behind the mixing desk (sooo cool!) when they suggested we took a trip down the pub so we all went along. They didn't seem to mind me being there and Dylan acted like it was cool so I went.

It seemed like the whole of the company was there and half of Kenton James plus Tony Macdonald and the lads and all sorts of liggers . . . these girls hanging around wearing London twatty fashion victim clothes and going off to the bogs every five minutes and coming back with runny noses. Smackheads! LOL. Oh my god and Kari Webster is such a cow! You would totally hate her and so would Ellie. But she's right in there with Dylan now. You should see the way she's all over him. Unbelievable.

Anyway, this is the biggie. I was at the table with Dyl and a couple of their lackies and then world war three happened. Macdonald came over and started talking really quiet with Dyl and then he said 'you have to' and Dyl just laughed and said 'no way' and then it got nasty. I kind of tuned in more as soon as I saw Dyl's face: you know what he's like when he goes off on one.

So Macdonald starts saying stuff like 'if you don't do it, we'll drop you' and 'you have no choice' and I get it what they're talking about: he's told Dylan they have to release Love Life Message as their first single!!!! Can you believe it? After everything Dyl's said about it and the riot at Spirit and how he's dissed Ellie?

Dylan started having a right go . . . he told them to fuck off and get another band if they didn't like it and stuff like that. Anyway, you could tell Macdonald wasn't having any of it, cos he just sort of hissed at Dyl. He said 'Ellie Batchelor could be making Love Life Message into the Christmas Number One right now. We're not sure, but we've heard a rumour. Do you want to come second to her again?'

Dyl just lost it. He was going on and on about Ellie and what she could do with her shit career and all that and then he said she couldn't do it anyway cos he'd written the song, it was his.

The next bit was the worst. I saw Andy looking over

187

and Macdonald said they should go somewhere quieter so they all kind of moved into a corner away from everybody else and I couldn't hear what was going on, but I could tell it was serious the way Dyl was reacting. He told me after what had happened. He was nearly crying, Kate, it was a nightmare.

Turns out that the contract they signed with Kenton James had a clause: publishing rights for existing material was signed over to some different company who can do what they want with the copyright. As owners of the rights, they can sell anybody the songs for the first six months of the Kenton James management deal and if Ellie wanted to do the song, she could do it, they had no way to stop her. So everything they've ever written belongs to this random 'third party' publishing company and BlackStar don't even own their own songs. They've been totally screwed.

I saw Dylan when he must have realised what it all meant. I could tell it had hit him like a brick in the face. He stood there looking like Andy did when he got twatted by those Sheffield United fans in Leeds that Saturday night a couple of years ago. He looked like he'd just suddenly lost all his fight. I've been worried about him since we got down here anyway, he doesn't look like he cares any more and he's started drinking again, maybe even doing coke, there's enough of it around. I'm scared shitless this is gonna put him over the edge again.

Anyway, in the end he's agreed to do it. Macdonald told him that if Ellie does make it her first single and she gets the hit, BlackStar will always be second best to her and they'll never catch up. Everyone will always think Ellie is the talent. And he persuaded Dylan that he needed to screw Ellie for everything she's supposed to have done to him and the band . . . when she left and nearly split them up. I tried to talk him out of it, but I guess they do need to try and use the song for themselves too. At least they'll get something from it.

Dyl's in his room at the hotel now and I'm on the computer in the lobby. I'm gonna get up there in a minute and try and sort something out, but I don't know what to do. He won't even talk to Andy and he's been in there all afternoon with the door locked. God knows what he's got in there.

Can you think of anything we can do, like maybe get to Ellie somehow? Do you think she would be able to help? BlackStar are recording the song tomorrow and releasing it on Monday, the same day

189

as Ellie if she does do it. I can't believe either of
them really would want all this to happen like it is,
if they knew. Is there any way we can find out if
she is? Her mobile's not working any more and I
tried emailing but it came back.

Anyway, let me know what you think. Call me. I just
hope wherever you are you're having a better time
than I am. I only came down to get the updates for
the papers on Pop World and BlackStar and now I'm
in the middle of a crisis.

Talk soon,
J xx

37

I had a girly night in on Thursday, not that I'd been out anywhere apart from the TV studios since I moved to the new hotel anyway. It was an amazing place though, complete luxury, five star plus, and I loved every minute of being on my own, focusing on just me and pampering myself with everything I could get my hands on using all the freebies in the bathroom.

I'd had a long day of rehearsing, but everything was really coming together with my songs. I'd decided to definitely do 'The Greatest Love of All' in the final as my first song, because it gave me a chance to demonstrate my range, plus all the grannies and mums would love it. Then I would nail the win with 'Love Life Message' for the teens, and especially the girls, as my second and final song.

Jansen, my vocal coach, was working with me on a Christina song that he thought I'd be doing, and I figured I must be doing a good job of pretending, because he hadn't twigged yet that I was faking. I'd even rigged up this weird dance routine for it with the choreographer, but I only put half my energy into it, knowing it'd never happen on the night. I'd also bombed my version of 'Love Life Message' in rehearsals earlier in the week just as planned, and Martin had promised that it would be exchanged at the last minute, just before the final on Saturday evening, so nobody would know what I was really doing.

I'd only spoken to Jayani once since Martin made his plans for me on Tuesday. She'd come to my dressing room soon after hearing that I wouldn't be doing 'Love Life Message' and somehow got past the ever-present Sandra, who must have been at the loo or something. Standing in the doorway, she gave me her usual huge smile and looked really happy to see me again, but worried she was going to get caught.

'How you doing, Ell?' she grinned. 'I'm so glad you're still here. This place is full of mental cases. You're the only normal person I can talk to. You made the right choice though. How's it going with the rehearsals?'

Jay was so open; I knew she was only asking because she cared. There was no edge to her at all, although she was nervously looking around to make sure we weren't going to get caught. I looked at her for a moment with real regret, wishing we could be as close as we had been before. Apart from Kate, she was one of the only real friends I'd ever made. But we were all working 'behind closed doors' now, with individual coaches, probably to stoke up the rivalry between us and make it seem more real to the viewers, and it had definitely had the effect of making me worry about what everybody else was doing. And Martin was right: no distractions. Everybody else was the enemy now. I decided I needed to cut this short.

'I'm fine. I'm sure you're fine too. Everything's fine. Now I'm sorry, but I need to focus. I can't talk. We'll catch up after the final if you want.'

I kept my eyes fixed on the mirror as I applied some more lipstick. I'd been a bitch before, but not like this. I glanced sideways to see Jayani's mouth fall open, her eyes widening further than even her make-up normally let them. She almost seemed to step backwards, as if she'd been punched.

'Right. Yeah. Erm, what's happened to you, Ell?'

I felt terrible, but at the same time, I knew it had to be done.

'I can't talk right now, Jay. Seriously. We have to focus for our own sakes now. We can get together after the show and catch up. Good luck, OK?'

I squeezed out a tiny smile and tried to will her to leave the room.

'What's going on, Ell?' she asked, confusion written all over her face. 'Why are you being like this?'

I stood up and faced her, across the threshold, starting to pull the door closed with my hand.

'Please, just go, Jay,' I said. I put my other hand out in front of me as a stop signal, keeping my expression blank to her questions.

'God,' she said, starting to see that I was serious. 'I thought you were different. You're just like all the others here, just out for yourself after all.'

I put my head down as she waited for me to deny it. I couldn't. It was true. But the difference was that I was going to win. She turned and started to walk away. I watched her go down the corridor until her footsteps faded and went back inside my dressing room, strangely content. It was good to be alone, knowing you had the edge, knowing you were heading towards your goal with nothing to distract you. I realised as I sat there that I'd never have been any good in a band, I needed to be a solo artist, to have my own space.

And now I had a whole suite to myself at the hotel and I was going to enjoy it: room service delivered a bottle of expensive white wine and a box of Belgian chocolates, and I settled in for the night. I was exhausted, but I was going to give myself the best relaxation a girl could get.

I threw on a thick, fluffy white robe, chose the 100 Greatest Love Songs channel on the suite's MP3 system with speakers in every room, and poured a glass of wine, before padding softly into the bathroom to sort out my night's entertainment. Soon there were bubbles everywhere and steam rising around the mirror as I plucked my eyebrows and applied a special Arabian Sea Deep Facial Cleansing Mask in bright turquoise. Then I jumped in the huge, steaming tub and settled in to relax.

It was heaven. It took a while but eventually I could feel myself nodding off, probably more to do with 'Lovely Day' by Bill Withers than the bath, but it wasn't really in the plan to drown, so I switched to shaving my legs and pits and generally tidying things up where they needed to be tidied.

Eventually everything seemed smooth enough, so I stood up, grabbed a couple of enormous lumps of fluff that the hotel called towels, wrapped myself up cosily and hit the bed for some chocolates and a rubdown with the moisturiser: Molton Brown Coco De Mer. Perfect.

I was halfway through the chocolates and just at the point where Bridget Jones realises she's left her diary for Colin Firth's character to read, when there was a knock at the door.

I jumped up and peered through the spyhole. It was Martin Harman, nervously checking that nobody had seen him at my door. It must be after eleven, I thought, he works too hard this guy, much harder than me. I needed to get better at that.

I opened up the door, apologising for being a bit red and splotchy from the heat of the bath still. He laughed briefly, seeming a little unsteady as he did, then regained his usual serious expression and stepped hastily inside. I noticed a faint smell of alcohol and extra strong mints as he spoke.

'Don't worry about that,' he said, as I cast around trying to clear up all my piles of relaxation material, his eyes moving carefully around the room as they always did. He was like a trained assassin, the Jason Bourne of entertainment, prepared for every surprise, even if he had been drinking. But it didn't make for a relaxed chat.

'I just called because I need to go through a couple of things about rehearsals and the plan for Saturday. I've also lined up a couple of interviews with some journalists I know for tomorrow, so that when you win on Saturday, there'll be in-depth stuff ready to go out when the Sundays hit the shops.' It was weird, I could smell the alcohol strongly now, but he wasn't slurring his words like a comedy drunk. The alcohol had definitely had an effect though: he sounded more American than English now, like he was speaking with an accent that wasn't his own. 'It's really important that we hit the ground running with every media outlet that we can if we're going to make the Christmas Number One slot.'

He paused, looking momentarily confused, so I jumped in.

'OK, cool. Erm, do you want to sit down? Have a chocolate . . .'

I offered him the mostly empty box. Perhaps if he ate something he might relax, and it might soak up some of the booze and then he might go. I didn't want him to stay for any longer than necessary, and I was fast losing my relaxed karma just by the way he was stepping from one foot to the other like he couldn't decide which one to rely on.

'Er, no, thanks. I'm trying to cut down.' He patted his stomach, which was completely flat, through an immaculately ironed shirt. I offered him a seat at my writing desk and I sat down on the edge of my bed, the only other place to sit in the room that wasn't twenty feet away. Even four feet seemed too close to me.

'So, who are the interviews with? I'm really excited about that. I like talking.'

I laughed and tried to focus on the job in hand. Avoiding a scene. He tried to smile.

'One's with Clare Davis, from the *Sunday News*, and the other is with *Late* magazine. I have a couple of writers down there who give me good stories in return for favours.' He winked.

I forced a laugh, which he seemed to believe in, and he visibly relaxed.

'Favours?' I asked, attempting to steer his mind away from a place I guessed he'd already started to go. 'Hope you're not breaking any rules, Martin. That would be bad.' I tried to joke, but it wasn't very convincing. He didn't seem to notice anyway.

'No, nothing too much, just a few priceless tickets for sold-out events here and there, the odd date with a beautiful escort, you know the kind of thing. There are a lot of beautiful women in London.'

He seemed to be sinking into his chair, his legs sliding further out between us. This wasn't a good sign. I waited for him to continue, aware that it was his job to make this conversation work, not mine, and if we ran out of things to say he might just go, but knowing that I couldn't risk offending him by asking him to leave, not now: not two days before the most important night of my life.

'You know, Ellie, I've been wanting to talk to you for a while now,' he continued, sliding back up the chair and leaning forward towards me a little, all of which seemed to be a bit of a struggle for him. 'On your own, I mean. I know

197

it's been really hard for you with everything that's happened over the last couple of months. You know, don't you, that if you ever need someone to talk to, you know, like an older brother figure, somebody who's been through a lot, you only have to ask.'

I couldn't decide whether to laugh or throw up. I steadied myself and held my voice firm.

' 'Course I know that, Martin. You've really helped with the song this week, and with getting everything organised.' I focused on work. I figured it was my only hope of avoiding what I could sense was coming.

'Yeah, yeah.' Harman seemed to drift off for a second, like he was lost in the conversation. Then he found himself again. 'I mean, helping you with the job is one thing, but there's much, much more I can offer. I'm experienced in a lot of ways, things to do with, well, more personal things.' He leaned forward across the space between us. It suddenly seemed much smaller than it should be, far too close for me. 'There are things I could do for you that we would both like.'

Suddenly he stood up straight and darted across the space between us, plonking himself heavily on to the bed beside me and leaning his face towards mine, his eyes slightly buggy and watery.

I smelled the alcohol more strongly now and I backed away, repulsed, feeling a surge of panic in my throat. He was a big man, much bigger than me. This was a bad situation, and I had to get myself out of it somehow, without blowing everything else completely. I pulled on all my reserves of strength. I'd faced down my dad. I could cope with this creep after that, surely?

I edged away, pretending it was making it easier to see his face as I spoke, but deliberately putting some more space between us.

'Martin, why don't we look at the song again? I really want your opinion on a new bit of melody I've worked out for the second chorus. I'll do it for you.'

I stood up quickly and moved to the sound equipment that lined the back wall of the room, switching on the amps and the CD player.

He looked over at me, trying to focus, wobbling now and holding himself up with a lot of difficulty. And it suddenly hit me. This man had obviously had to make one hell of an effort to control the effects of the alcohol since he'd been in my room so that he could get even as far as my bed. He must have had a lot more to drink than I'd thought. He looked pretty shit-faced now to be honest, and all the effort was obviously becoming just too much to keep up.

So, I bet he wouldn't remember all this in the morning.

'I don't want to hear you sing, Ellie, I want you to come over here and sit down next to me.' The fake American accent was turning quickly to a mushy, drunken slur. His head was starting to wobble, like it was too heavy for his neck. Maybe my chocolates had pushed him over the edge? I suddenly saw Harman, the great, powerful, popular figure the public and he himself imagined, for what he really was: a tired old perv on the make. He was pathetic, not even capable of abusing his position properly. I decided to take a chance, pretty sure it would pay off.

I turned the mike on and spoke softly, like I was stroking him with my voice.

'Martin, this is a test. Is that hair all yours, or are you wearing a wig?'

Harman stared back at me without answering, obviously unable to reply. He'd passed the test brilliantly. I continued.

'Martin, do exactly as I say as soon as I've finished. I want you to get your ugly, ignorant, dickless, talentless old arse out of my bedroom right now, and stop trying to force yourself into my pants, because if you don't, I'm going to turn this microphone up and shout so loud that the whole eighth floor of this hotel will hear that same sentence all over again, perfectly. And when they do, your wonderful career will be over, and the Sunday papers will really have a story then, won't they?'

He looked across at me and seemed to find some focus for a second, finally, before losing me in the fog that was growing in the room.

'Ellie?' he questioned, obviously not sure what he was hearing.

'And we'll never mention this again, will we?'

I didn't wait for an answer, I knew what it would be, what it had to be, for his own sake, even if he had followed everything I'd said. He stumbled to his feet and tried to stand still in front of me for a moment, trying to become what he believed himself still to be. But he knew it was pointless. I was too strong, too certain, too sober. His head wobbled downwards as he mumbled something incomprehensible into his shoulder, before he trudged across the room without looking back and let himself quietly out of the door, a defeated, sad little figure.

I grasped the microphone tightly, before pulling it off the stand and throwing it at the door with a clank of reverb and noise, leaving no mark on the heavy door, but a huge dent in the mike that somebody else would have to pay for. Martin Harman probably. And then I sank to my knees, curling myself up into a protective ball, wrapping myself even tighter inside my fluffy white gown.

So much for 'me time' and keeping the focus.

They were all gonna get it on Saturday, every last one of them.

38

KENTON JAMES AGENCY
<u>Internal e-Memo</u>: (<u>Highly Confidential</u>)
<u>Circulation: S Kenton; T Macdonald; M Harman;</u>
<u>From:</u> Tony Macdonald
<u>To:</u> Martin Harman
<u>Cc:</u> Steve Kenton
<u>Subject:</u> BlackStar/Ellie Batchelor

Martin,

Thanks for the note about Saturday's final. With
'Love Life Message' now in place for both artists,
we all stand to benefit on this either way.
For our part, Steve and the partners have briefed
Pop World on procedures to cover all eventualities
re: voting control and ensuring the Batchelor
win. We're assured that camera angles, sets,
lighting, interviews, etc. will all favour her. Thanks
for the heads-up on the various obstacles you've
put in place for the others! Nice creative work

there, as we'd expect!

Voting lines will be tightly controlled. From our end, just to clarify, votes will appear to be registered for the other contestants, but only one in three will actually appear in the final totals.

So the business: 'Love Life Message' to be released almost simultaneously by both BlackStar (10am) and Ellie Batchelor (10.30) on Monday morning. We will hold our press conference at the Dorchester. Yours is booked for the Hammersmith as agreed. Advertising as follows in brief:

- TV ads: 'Christmas is no time for dancing . . . Batchelor v BlackStar: World War Three! etc.' You've seen the storyboarding.
- Print media: Interviews with the band are sorted. Most had to be ghost-written but we are using earlier quotes from Patrick to further stoke the conflict. We understand you have various outlets ready to run with the feud story from the Batchelor side?
- Internet: Official sites ready to go live at the press conferences: you can launch right after the final if you prefer: might cover our tracks a bit.
- Bus shelters/Underground stations/billboards: *Batchelor: the selected semi-nudes from the Da Silva shoot last month plus the caption: 'This means everything to me: boys, don't cry . . .'

* BlackStar: Kari Webster fore-fronted, the guitarist and bassist sitting behind, captioned: 'WarStar?-BlackStar?-RealStar.'

- Media appearances are booked all week for both artists, culminating with the chart announcement on Sunday. Both artists to be available on the phone to the studio at that moment, obviously only the Number One artist will be interviewed. I'll leave Batchelor to you for that.

Returns from the music stores and online suggest that demand for both singles will be unprecedented as noted. With no official news of the Batchelor single yet, the rumours in the press have created huge interest, which is only adding to the hype. We anticipate either one will take the top spot, as predicted, because pre-sale figures are already running at 10 to 1 in favour of our artists against any other release in December.
We're pleased with the product and the project, Martin, and it's been a pleasure to work with you. Once everything is concluded, we'll look forward to working with you again. It's been a highly productive experience for all of us already and we're looking forward to those sales figures already! Obviously, should BlackStar prevail, I will step aside as we agreed for you to continue with their

management until they become surplus to your needs. Kari Webster is returning to us in the new year anyway, and I'm sure your use of Ellie Batchelor will run its course in time.

Just a quick personal note: I'll be wintering for some weeks in Monte Carlo on my yacht. It would be great to see you down there. Champagne and money-counting sounds good to me!

So, in seasonal anticipation of a lovely Christmas bonus for all of us on the project,

Tony.

39

'Welcome back to the *Pop World* studios in London, everybody.'

The applause started to die down as Keeley Bryant, *Pop World* presenter and former children's TV star, started to speak. She was wearing a stunning sequinned gown that looked like something out of a science fiction movie and when I'd seen her in make-up I'd wondered if there'd be enough left for the rest of us. But she was a professional and she seemed to be on my side.

'So, you've heard her once this evening with a beautiful, beautiful version of the classic Whitney Houston song "The Greatest Love of All", and she had me in tears back there. I can tell you that doesn't happen very often.' She stepped back and shifted from her front foot, sweeping her long blonde hair extensions back over her shoulders. 'Well, not unless I've lost my lip-gloss before the show!' she shouted back into the mike.

The audience broke into huge peals of laughter that washed round the studio. I peered out from the gloom and wondered, not for the first time in the series, how I'd ended up here. Keeley carried on bravely through the hilarity she'd created.

'But now we're in for something special. I'm so excited about this, and it's a surprise for all of us, because Ellie is back with the song that the nation took to our hearts back in October. She's kept it a secret all week, even from the team here, but all is about to be revealed. So, with the stunning "Love Life Message", it's the gorgeous Ellie Batchelor!'

I walked out to what seemed like a huge roar of applause and cheering. I could just make out my dad in the audience, to the right behind the judges, and Kate and Jamie were there too, looking a little sheepish when the cameras rolled round at them, I imagined, but clapping wildly right now. It seemed like a bigger and better reception than I'd had for weeks, and it gave me so much confidence.

The spotlight focused in on me, reducing to a tiny circle that held my face suspended in the darkness, as the piano and strings intro blended with the rhythms I'd once created on my computer at home, just a bit more professional sounding now. It was a beautiful song, and I couldn't wait to sing it, and after my intensive work on it all week, I knew it would be fantastic. I had three and a half minutes to convince the country to vote for me: this was my chance and I wasn't going to blow it. The first song had been a taster, a warm-up, but this was where I would kill it and where my future began. By Monday I would be a pop star with a single for sale on CD or download, a career in music, the life that

I'd always wanted. Maybe I wouldn't be going to Glastonbury, but I would be up on a stage being worshipped. Who cared about Glastonbury?

The song only seemed to take seconds to sing, but I knew I'd given the performance of my life. There was a hard ball of love and hate and fear and passion in my chest as I finished, and I almost felt like collapsing with the emotion of the past few days and weeks. There had been tears pricking in my eyes as I'd sung my favourite lines:

> *'I've laid down, and I don't want to fake it any more,*
> *I've spoken, and woken up to an empty room,*
> *And I don't want to spend my time,*
> *Chasing after last year's prize,*
> *I'm heading for a breakthrough of my very own*
> *Looking on the bright side of my silver moon*
> *Looking over all the things I thought I'd never own,*
> *And now I'm coming home.'*

As I'd sung them, I thought of Dylan and Andy and the day I first heard that song back in Andy's room with the window open and the Yorkshire sunlight filling that simple space, Andy's posters of half-naked girls on the wall and Dylan's gorgeous hands when he picked out the notes for me on his guitar. I remembered Andy grinning because he knew that there was something special going on, something none of us had ever experienced before, and I could feel the song becoming more powerful with every line, every thought turning it into something very special for me, and for the audience.

And I thought of my mum in Leeds watching me, willing me to win maybe, but mostly willing me to have my own life and break free of anything that was holding me back, making me too much like her, too locked into her regrets, her missed opportunities, her terrible decisions.

Trembling with emotion as I finished, I took the applause and the cheering from the studio audience. Keeley Bryant was trying to shush them, to let the judges speak, but the whole crowd was standing and whistling, shouting. She couldn't get them to stop. I pulled myself together to focus on the judges' comments, grinning insanely at every compliment, laughing warmly at Martin Harman's assessment of my future as a world superstar in the same bracket as some people I didn't want to be compared to, until the segment was over and I could see the floor manager giving the sign to wind it up to Keeley. She took my hand, and hugged me, before asking me how I felt.

'I'm so excited,' I laughed. 'I bet you can all see my knees trembling I'm so nervous.' I looked down beyond my short minidress to my knees, and did a fake, extra-trembling knee-knock for the cameras. I got a big whoo from the audience and faked horror. I thought back to Martin's final instructions. He was right every time, despite his sleaziness. At least he'd never mentioned Thursday night again.

'So, Ellie, you've decided that "Love Life Message" will be your first single? Should you win, of course. How does it feel to know you could be working with Martin Harman's label by Monday?' She flashed a massive brilliant white toothy grin at me as she spoke, seeming to suggest that it was practically a done deal.

'It's amazing. I talked to Martin yesterday about songs and gave him my ideas, and he agreed with me that this was the best song for me to do, the one that means the most. I just love it.'

Keeley glanced away for a second to the floor manager and then wrapped up the little chat with a girlie giggle.

'I'll buy it!' she laughed. 'It's brilliant . . .' There was another huge burst of applause as she hugged me again, something I'd never seen her do once before with any contestant, before leading me off stage and passing me on to the stage manager who was lurking in the shadows.

Soon I was being propelled by hands I didn't know, attached to faces I couldn't see, through a tunnel of people speaking words that didn't make sense, until finally the door of my dressing room shut behind me and I was all alone again. I slumped down in my chair and closed my eyes. What a performance! I'd done it . . . everything I'd set out to do. I felt sure I would win now, nothing could stop me.

I glanced up at the television monitor suspended from the wall in the corner of the room. Keeley Bryant was talking to the judges and numbers were passing across the screen to show viewers how to vote for me, Jayani and Jermaine. There would now be a thirty-minute break for the news before *Pop World* came back and the winner was announced.

Time to chill and think about what might happen. Time to pray, I thought to myself, and to get my make-up sorted for the winner's performance.

40

I put my headphones in and zoned out the world. It was how I always dealt with this bit of time in the show, when there was nothing left for me to do but wait, and nobody was allowed into the dressing-room area except the judges and the minders. To be honest, I quite liked it: finally I had time to come down and stop worrying, and the time passed quickly this way. Sometimes I put old BlackStar stuff on my MP3 that I'd downloaded from their website. Today was no different. It gave me time to think and something inspiring to listen to while I did it.

I lay back on my own personal sofa and drifted away, thoughts still spinning round about the reception I'd received from the audience. I couldn't believe it. It had felt like I was floating on a warm, thick, gooey gloop of love, and I'd loved every minute of it. I felt like it had proved me right about 'going solo', as Kate had once called it as a joke. But she was right: I was alone, and I was making everything happen for me, without any interference from my dad, BlackStar, anybody. Well, except Martin Harman, and I had him where I wanted him now too.

Pretty soon I was drifting into a daydream, and long minutes passed in a hazy imagining of happy futures and adoring fan worship.

I woke up when the five-minute warning bell rang loudly from its position over the door, breaking into 'Mush Mush', an old favourite of mine with a dance vibe that Dylan and I had written one night when we were drunk. Five minutes, and I would know whether all my dreams were going to come true. Butterflies immediately started fluttering around my tummy again and I got up to stretch and redo my hair.

Suddenly I became aware of a lot of commotion outside my door. There was banging against the wall and the sound of voices shouting and arguing. What the hell was going on? Should I go out there? We'd been told never to leave during the voting break, only when our minders came to get us.

Then I heard a voice I recognised.

'Ellie? Ellie, open the door . . .' It was muffled, but I could pick Jamie's voice out anywhere, I'd heard him talk more than anybody I knew.

There was another bang against the door, more heavy this time and scary for it, and I wondered if the door might give in. I looked up at the clock: four minutes to ten. What if Jamie was in trouble?

Then I heard his voice again. 'Get off me, I need to talk to her . . .'

I grasped the door handle and tried it. It was locked. On the outside.

I panicked. With all my strength I pulled on the handle, trying to force the lock. Who'd locked me in? This wasn't funny. The door gave towards me slightly, only a tiny bit, but it was obviously only caught on a lock that wasn't too strong. I tugged again, this time putting all my effort and weight behind it. Suddenly, the door burst open, just as I'd moved to the side, and Jamie was sprawled on the floor of my dressing room, a security guard in uniform lying next to him.

Jamie was first to react.

'Ellie, I've got to talk to you. It's important. Andy has just texted me and we had to find you.'

I tried to work out what he was on about. And what did he mean 'we'? I looked back out of the doorway to see Kate against the corridor wall held back in the arms of another security guard. I heard her for the first time too, but she was muffled by the guard's arms around her head.

'What the hell's going on, Jamie? I've got to go on in a minute.' I thought hard for a millisecond. 'You're freaking me out. What's Andy got to do with it? Are they just trying to wreck everything for me again?'

I heard myself shouting through my confusion and a voice seemed to jump into my head saying 'calm down, you don't want to ruin your voice'. Suddenly, four or five more security guards and a couple of members of the production team streamed into my dressing room, filling it up in moments, grabbing Jamie by the arms and legs and shouting orders at each other.

Jamie struggled up so I could still see his eyes. They were

214

crazed. What was he doing? What did he have to say that was so important?

I called out to the guards. 'What are you doing? Put him down, he's my friend.'

But they were already half out of the door, Jamie's legs jamming against one of the door frames for a second, before it was lifted free and he was on his way again. I jumped after him into the doorway, to find Sandra blocking the way. She wasn't a big woman, but her arms were strong and she wasn't going to move them when I tried to force her.

'Stay here,' she said firmly. 'You're on in two minutes. Final call. Do you want to let some lunatic ruin this and end up back where you started again?'

I tried to see past her, through her looming presence in front of me.

'He's not a lunatic,' I shouted. 'He's my friend.' I called out again. 'Jamie! What's happening?'

Just audibly, I heard him splutter out a few words, before a hand must have been clamped over his mouth.

'It's all a set-up, Ell. They stole the song from Dyl and it's not his either now. They're just using you all to make mon—'

And then he was cut off. Half a second later, a door slammed a little way off and they were all gone.

I tried to see where he was so I could follow, or at least trace where they had taken them, but the corridor was strangely normal again and they were nowhere to be seen. Suddenly quiet, it seemed as though nothing had happened, as though I'd imagined everything. I felt a horrible chill run through me. Production staff criss-crossed this way and that. The only reminder of what had just happened was Sandra's body and arms blocking my way, and my mind was gripped by a sense of total confusion.

Just then, Martin Harman stepped out from behind the vending machine that never had chocolate in it, the one that had hummed next to my dressing room for ten weeks now.

'It's time for you to get on stage now, Ellie, and complete the job in hand. You're nearly there, and I can't wait to start working with you next week. Ignore that little interruption, he's just jealous, probably sent by your old "friends",' he emphasised the sarcasm of his word as he spoke, 'to put you off.'

I stared at him through my confusion as the one-minute warning bell sounded. I couldn't work it out. What if Dylan and Andy really had sent Jamie to sabotage me? I wouldn't put it past Dyl to do that, not after everything he'd been saying and doing recently. But why Jamie? Jamie had never taken sides. He'd always stayed close to all of us. He'd been writing my website blogs up until a couple of weeks ago too.

'Come on. I can't wait to hear you sing again.'

Harman smiled and held out his hand, as Sandra moved to one side to let me pass. I moved quickly back into my room and tried to block out the events of the last few minutes. I would deal with it after the show, whatever it was. Now I had to get out there and be professional, get the prize I deserved at last.

I fixed my hair hurriedly in the full-length mirror and smoothed down my clothes. Sandra quickly moved me through the stage door as Harman took his place with the other judges. Just then, Jayani appeared from nowhere to stand beside me in the wings. I'd barely even noticed her all week, let alone her performance tonight, and we hadn't spoken since we'd fallen out. She looked good though, I had to admit it.

'Good luck,' she smiled, nervously. She looked like she needed some reassurance. 'Whatever happened before, I still wouldn't mind if you won, Ell. You were amazing tonight.'

I nodded quickly and looked away.

It wasn't the time for making up. I had a job to do.

41

The *Pop World* music thundered noisily around us, as a panning camera soared and dipped like a bird of prey from one side of the stage to the other in front of us, and we stood together, Jayani, Jermaine and me, the three of us waiting for the final results, our destiny.

Keeley Bryant talked to the audience from just in front of the podiums we were perched on like Olympic runners, lined up to receive our medals. I was terrified. I felt a bit of a prat standing there anyway, and I didn't know what sort of pose to do, so I just sort of hung, feeling exhausted, confused, exhilarated, anything but focused. Try as I might to stop it, the incident with Jamie and Kate kept invading my thoughts.

I could see the three empty seats where my dad, Jamie and Kate had been sitting. Why wasn't my dad there now? What the hell was going on? In between my questions I heard flashes of Keeley and her build-up to the announcement.

'OK, so the voting is now over, the lines are closed. We'll be announcing the results in reverse order, starting with the third-placed finalist, in just a few moments' time. But just before we do, guys, we want to show you some of your best bits, some of your incredible journeys, from the first audition, to our home visits, right through to today. So good luck to all of you, and we'll start with you, Jayani.'

Keeley turned and gestured to us to turn, and we joined her by wheeling round to face the massive screen that lit up with Jayani's face. They played some uplifting ballad that had something to do with what we were watching, and we saw Jayani's life over the last three months unfold in front of us.

I stared at the screen in a haze, taking nothing in, trying to come up with some sort of explanation for Jamie's actions, my dad's absence from the audience. He would never miss this. He only ever missed things he thought I wouldn't win, and that had only happened twice in my entire childhood.

Jayani's journey ended and Jermaine's began. I was getting nowhere, but what if there was no reason to be worried? Maybe it was what I'd thought before? Maybe Dylan was just using Jamie to get back at me after all?

I clicked into focus as I heard my name and then my face flashed up in front of us, the face of Ellie Batchelor, the girl from Leeds, back in the time when I knew who I was. My heart seemed to miss a beat as the images began to roll, backed up by 'Beautiful' by Christina Aguilera. I'd always loved that song anyway, and the words and music, combined with pictures of my audition and all that confidence, my hair in one of the many BlackStar styles and a complete lack of make-up, seemed to take me back in time and away from this ice-cold, air-conditioned studio full of people I didn't know.

I saw my mum in images from the home visit they'd done just after Boot Camp, and my house, the garden, the street I used to walk down to school and to Andy's and Dyl's. There was Leeds city centre, the Corn Exchange and all my favourite cool shops in a circle around the café where we used to meet to have all-day breakfasts when we hung out in town on a Saturday afternoon.

I watched my transformation from the confident girl I used to be into the confused young woman I was now. I thought about Andy and the night we kissed: I'd been confused then as well, despite his lovely, gentle, thoughtful kisses, and then I thought of Harman and all the touching, the suggestive comments, the secret agreement. No confusion there, not now. But the pictures on the screen told their own story, and now they were all from the show, my performances, the coaching, the rehearsal room. They were what I'd become, and I couldn't deny that it was all inside of me too: this new girl, the one styled by other people, dressed by a department, organised by a team.

Jamie's words came back into my head again as the final few bars of the song played, and they showed the end of tonight's performance of 'Love Life Message' and the incredible ovation I got. I couldn't help myself. Tears started to fill my eyes. I imagined twenty different cameras homing in on them and me from every angle, picking up on my emotions and capturing them, feeding them to the whole country, everybody taking their little bit of me like I was a meal to be eaten up and digested, to satisfy their appetites.

I wiped the beginnings of the tears away quickly with my fingers, careful not to ruin my make-up. It was time to pull myself together again, for one last time. I'd got this far, done most of what I'd set out to do, and now I was going to find out if I'd achieved my dream. I had to focus, to commit.

Keeley was already talking.

'So, here it is. Quiet please, everyone in the studio. Oh the tension in here is unbearable. Can somebody get me a towel and rub me down?' She laughed with the audience as the atmosphere was pierced just for a second.

'Right, here goes.' She read from a card in her hand. 'In the greatest ever competition in *Pop World* history, we have had more votes for this final than ever before, up by three million votes on last year.' There was a spontaneous burst of applause, led by the enthusiastic floor manager, before Keeley quietened everybody again. A few whoops and shouts were heard before the audience fell silent.

'In a few seconds, the picture of our third-place winner will appear on the big screen.' An insistent, pulsing piece of music filled the studio and graphics filled the screen, ticking us down to zero. Jayani, Jermaine and I stared at the screen, unblinking, holding each other's hands.

Suddenly Jermaine's face appeared and the crowd

erupted. I breathed in and composed myself in the mayhem.

In a matter of seconds, Jermaine was interviewed, cheered again, reassured and was off the stage and out of the way. It seemed like they just wanted to focus on the final announcement. Part of me felt bad for him. The other part wanted to get on with it too.

'Guys, can you come down here and stand with me, just here.' Keeley positioned Jayani and me on either side of her, her arms around our shoulders hugging us tightly. The judges nodded at us, Harman particularly trying to get my attention. I looked away from them and again noticed the empty seats where my friends had been. Keeley snapped me back to attention.

'OK, guys, ten seconds from when I finish speaking, the picture of the winner of *Pop World 2008* will appear on the screen behind us. In a moment we'll turn around and the countdown will begin. Have you guys anything you want to say before we do?'

Jayani looked across at me and smiled nervously, as I chewed on my bottom lip with my front teeth. 'I just want to say to everybody out there that I've loved every minute of *Pop World* and thanks to everyone who voted for me, whatever happens.' She looked again at me. 'And it's been great being here with you, Ell, too. Good luck.'

After I'd dropped her like a stone, she was still prepared to be nice. I smiled and looked back at her, seeing her almost for the first time again as my friend. I reached across the front of Keeley and grabbed her hand. 'You too, Jay, you're brilliant, and I'm so glad it's you and me up here together for this.'

I wondered if I could manage to be like that one day? I made these friends, and they seemed to stay loyal to me, no matter what I did. Like Jamie, and Kate, and Jayani. But what about Dylan and Andy? What if Jamie was trying to tell me something from them that would help me? What if they still cared for me like Jayani did, and we could make it all better somehow?

Keeley held us tight again and spoke.

'OK, it's time to hear who will be this year's *Pop World* winner. Let's turn and face the music, girls.'

We swivelled round and the music started again, pounding and running, building for ten seconds that seemed to last for ever.

And then the picture appeared on the screen.

42

The audience went crazy, and fireworks and lights and noise and crashes seemed to be going on all around us, as if it was Bonfire Night and New Year's Eve rolled into one. Cameras were darting quickly around the stage and all I could hear were the sounds of people cheering and shouting, calling out my name.

It was me. I'd done it.

For a few seconds I felt like I was going mad. I couldn't stop jumping up and down on the spot shouting 'Yes!' over and over again. Jayani was somewhere there hugging me. So was Keeley Bryant. I thought about my mum at home, probably hugging herself, tears running down her face, all alone but happy for me at least.

I couldn't take it all in. In fact, the only images I could focus on were of how other people would be feeling. Dad? Kate and Jamie? And what about Dylan and Andy. Would anybody be happy for me? I kept smiling and jumping up and down, but inside I was in turmoil. Jamie was just like Jayani, loyal to the last. There was no way he had been trying to put me off before. He was helping me with something about the song.

But it was mayhem on stage, people running everywhere just off camera, the judges coming to congratulate me and commiserate with Jayani. I was getting covered in glittery bits of paper that were all through the air like a rainfall of Christmas tinsel, sticking to my hot face and head in the strangest places, and I couldn't think clearly at all.

Over the din of the studio noise, I heard Keeley shouting her final goodbyes to the studio audience and those at home.

'It's been an amazing finale and a great series, everybody, and thanks for all your votes. By a huge margin, a star is born. So, here she is again, with her brand-new single, "Love Life Message", to be released on Monday and available in all good record shops and online, here's your amazing *Pop World* winner, the incredible . . . Ellie Batchelor!'

She stepped to one side and held out her arms to give me the stage. Suddenly, everybody began to float into the distance and pan away, and in a moment, I was left alone, in the middle of the stage, with just the noise and the little glittery things around me. I heard the opening bars of 'Love Life Message' start to play, and automatically sensed my body preparing to sing, like a robot programmed to perform. I took a deep breath, and looked for the microphone, which began to rise magically out of the stage a few metres in front of me.

I closed my eyes to shut out the chaos, and breathed deeply. Suddenly I was able to focus on me again, like the music had opened a channel back to who I really was. An image flashed in front of my eyes of another stage a long time ago, and far away from here. It was the little stage at the Spirit, dirty, wooden and dingy, with the club lights that used to spin over the dance floor; and the basic sound system that Dylan used to set up as best he could to make us sound like we were professionals; and the crowd in front of us, people of my age, mates from school, lads and girls from around the scene who knew that we were something special, something worth checking out; and my friends behind me in the band as I moved forward to sing the same song I was going to do now, the first time we performed it, properly, like it was meant to be.

I stepped forward to the microphone as the music gave me my cue to sing and I moved so that my mouth was positioned perfectly, as I'd been taught to do, to breathe out the first few words. The audience looked on transfixed, the judges still congratulating themselves on my victory in front of me and Keeley Bryant crouching to the side of a camera on the studio floor and waiting expectantly.

And I kept my mouth shut and my cue passed me by.

The music kept playing, but I didn't sing a word.

I stared into the audience as signs of puzzlement started to form on the faces of the production staff and the judges. I saw the floor manager waving frantically at the sound guy and suddenly the music stopped and restarted at the beginning and I stepped forward again to the microphone.

'No, could you stop the music please?' I said calmly. 'Just stop it.'

A couple more bars of 'Love Life Message' played, before it stopped awkwardly in the middle of a phrase and there was total silence. I could see the floor manager speaking urgently into his face mike, his hand cupped around it to hide his words.

'Something's wrong,' I started, softly. 'I don't know what it is, but this just doesn't feel right. It's felt wrong for weeks, but I've tried to cover it up and bury it and make it go away. But I can't.' I stopped to catch my breath, and tried to ignore the threads of doubt that were still gnawing away at my insides. I was speaking to twenty million people right now. I tried to imagine them all naked, but it didn't help much. So much for coaching.

I spoke again, trying to sound confident.

'There's all this stuff going on inside me about whether I should be doing this and whether it's right for me, and I've realised that it isn't. And I can't go on pretending any more. I'm just a girl from Leeds who sings in a band. I'm not a diva or a pop star, I'm me, and I've forgotten what that feels like and I want it back.' I paused again, checking that the floor manager wasn't moving to cut transmission. I wanted everybody to hear my words now. This did feel right, finally.

'*Pop World*'s great, but it's not for me, because it's what they want me to be, not what I am. And I've been singing this amazing song for weeks here, thinking that my old band would be OK about it all in the end and that I had the right.

But I don't, really.' I hesitated for a second, biting the inside of my mouth and frowning a bit as I looked around the studio. Everybody was listening still. Maybe they hadn't cut me off because it made better TV than me singing?

'I want to give "Love Life Message" back to my friends. I can't sing it or release it as a single, because it's not really mine, it's only a bit mine. If anything, I guess it kind of belongs to all of us together, but it belongs to Dylan Patrick mostly, cos he wrote most of it. So I hope you'll buy their single.' I looked up towards the back row of the studio and then right at the camera in front of me with the red light on. 'The band is called BlackStar and they're brilliant, and it comes out on Monday.'

I stopped and looked down at my outfit, and gripped the sides of the floaty short skirt with my fingers and pulled them out horizontal to my thighs.

'All this, it's not me,' I said, stepping out of my strappy, ridiculously high-heeled pointy shoes and moving down on to the stage floor in my bare feet. I picked up the shoes and got up on tiptoes to reach the microphone again. For a second the operator automatically moved it up and down a bit until we came to a compromise about the best position for me to still reach it.

'So I'm giving back my win. I hope you don't hate me for this and I'm so grateful to everybody for voting for me, but I can't do it, I just can't do it. I don't belong on *Pop World*.' I stopped again and waited, wondering what to do next. I'd said everything I wanted to say now. I glanced up and gave them an apologetic half-smile. 'Erm, I'm going now, anyway. Sorry.'

I gripped the shoes into both my hands and ran across the polished floor towards the stage exit on the left, my bare feet hardly disturbing the heavy silence in the studio.

Nobody said a word to me as I passed through the backstage area. In a few moments I heard the familiar sound of the *Pop World* theme tune begin again, and I was alone, back in my dressing room, exhausted.

43

Daily Herald
Tuesday

THE GREAT ROCK AND ROLL SCANDAL

Days after an astonishing finale to this year's hit TV show Pop World *in which the winning contestant, Ellie Batchelor, 18, from Leeds, declined her prize, revelations about potentially fraudulent backstage activities continue to emerge.*

Television and music industry watchdogs are today investigating allegations that the programme's voting was rigged throughout the series' twelve-week run, and that secret contracts were drawn up to manipulate musical product and chart positions both of artists involved in the programme and others outside it. There are even suggestions that young artistes were being set up to take part in a battle for the coveted and extremely lucrative Christmas Number One slot, and that performers were duped into singing away their rights for potentially valuable publishing rights to their own songs.

On the latter charge, Martin Harman, pop-music 'Svengali' to the Pop World stable of artists, has been implicated in the scandal at some level, although programme makers and investigators declined to comment on his involvement yesterday. Harman himself released a media statement in which he declared: 'I have nothing to hide. Everything I do for my artistes is in their best interests. I challenge these so-called investigators to prove their unpleasant and libellous accusations. "Put up, or shut up" is my message to them. And meanwhile, I will continue to work hard on the careers of my artistes and for the good of the great British public and their entertainment.'

Harman has powerful supporters in the music industry both in Europe and America, and media analysts suggest that it would be unlikely that a case against him could be proven, despite previous unsubstantiated rumours of past indiscretions with contestants on the reality music show that he created, developed and exported around the world.

In a dramatic twist yesterday, one of the two artistes involved, BlackStar, a band from the Leeds area with a growing national following, asked fans NOT to buy their single and instead to donate their money to the 'Keep Music Real' campaign. Dylan Patrick, Andy Moffat and Kari Webster issued their statement through lawyers that they are consulting about existing contracts with the Kenton James Agency (alleged in the USA to have links to Harman's own global corporate organisation). Their spokesperson added that they are co-operating fully with the watchdog's enquiries.

Ellie Batchelor, meanwhile, is said to be with friends and family and reconsidering her future plans. No replacement 'winner' of Pop World has been announced, and a production company source admits that there is 'some doubt' as to whether the programme can survive this current crisis.

Epilogue

The small, cramped tour bus, more of a big camper van really, was divided into two sections: seating at the front, a toilet and a couple of bunk beds at the back.

Through the stained windows, another northern industrial landscape could just be seen, dirty-green trees dotting themselves heroically between factory plots and endless concrete road intersections.

Two young guys sat hunched over their guitars, clearly finding it difficult to pick over some chords that were not fitting together as they would like.

'You need to do a D minor there, Dyl,' the first said. He was taller, more broad and muscular than the other, his hair much shorter.

'No way. If we do the D minor there, then how can we still have the bridge with the E?'

The second was dressed in faded denim, virtually head to toe, completely out of fashion according to the magazines that littered the table between them, but actually right back in it, for just that reason.

'Are we actually in Bolton yet, Andy?' Dylan asked. His

curly fringe flopped right down over his guitar, so that people often wondered if it would end up getting caught in the strings.

Andy looked up for a minute and out of the window.

'I dunno,' he said. 'But when we get to the venue I'm going out for fish and chips. I'm starving. Don't care how far we are away from one. It's a right dump, is that place. They'll only have pork scratchings if we're lucky.'

'Pork scratchings and warm beer and about twelve people in the audience if we're lucky,' Dylan laughed. 'Unless we've been forgiven here as well.'

They caught each other's eyes for a moment and nodded knowingly, caught in thoughts they both seemed to understand without speaking. There was shared history between them, and they trusted one another completely.

Dylan snapped out of his thoughts first, drawn by the moaning sound of somebody waking from a long sleep and making sure everybody else knew about it.

'She's up,' he said, nodding towards the sleeping compartment behind Andy.

'About time too,' Andy laughed. 'We'll have a new album ready by the time she's ready to crawl out of her pit.'

He turned to look in the same direction as Dylan.

From underneath a mud-coloured blanket a pair of tanned, toned arms snaked their way out, stretching and contorting in a sort of arm-dance that the boys both enjoyed for a second or two too long.

'What are you two doing?' the girl's voice called out,

muffled still by the blanket and the edge of sleep. 'Are we nearly there yet?'

Dylan and Andy laughed.

'You've been asleep for about four hours, so yeah, we're nearly there. And we need some help on a chord and some harmonies, if you think you can get out here before we reach Carlisle on Saturday?'

The girl writhed sideways in her bunk and then slid slowly off it on to the floor, before finding her feet and standing up to stretch herself out one more time. She was wearing khaki combats and a tight strappy top with scribbled gold writing on the front, and her black hair was messed up by the uncomfortable sleep she'd just endured. She slipped on some battered size-ten men's trainers over her bare feet and took the small step that led into the seating area.

'OK, play it for me. Then I'll make it better,' she laughed and Andy lightly punched her on the arm.

The two boys started to strum and Dylan sang the tune to words that made no sense at all just yet. That would come in time. For now the chords and the melody were coming, and it was enough that the three of them were here together making music together.

Ellie smiled as the sounds filled the inside of the bus, and her head began to fill with the buzz of a hundred new ideas for the song.